A Small Civil War

A SMALL
CIVIL WAR

BY
John Neufeld

Atheneum Books for Young Readers

Atheneum Books for Young Readers
An imprint of Simon & Schuster Children's Publishing Division
1230 Avenue of the Americas
New York, New York 10020

Book design by PIXEL PRESS

The text of this book is set in Monotype Bembo.

First Edition
Printed in the United States of America
10 9 8 7 6 5 4 3 2 1

Also available in an Aladdin Paperbacks edition.

Library of Congress Cataloging-in-Publication Data
Neufeld, John.
A small civil war / by John Neufeld.—1st ed.
p. cm.
Summary: When thirteen-year-old Georgia joins a crusade to fight
the proposed banning of *The Grapes of Wrath* from her school
library, she is shocked when other members of her family
do not share her passion for the cause.
ISBN 0-689-80770-8
[1. Censorship—Fiction.] I. Title.
PZ7.N4425Sm 1996
[Fic]—dc20
96-2030

Other Books for Young Readers
by John Neufeld

Edgar Allan
Lisa, Bright and Dark
Touching ("Twink")
Sleep Two, Three, Four!
Freddy's Book
For All the Wrong Reasons
Sunday Father
Sharelle
Almost a Hero
Gaps in Stone Walls

A Small Civil War

Chapter 1

Georgia Van Buren, thirteen, newly in eighth grade, ran every day on emergency power.

What to other people were merely problems, at worst stumbling blocks along a day's progress, to Georgia—red of hair, blue of eye, fair of complexion—were alarm bells in a firehouse. Before anyone else in her family knew what was happening, Georgia was sliding down the shiny steel pole ready to leap aboard the fire engine and race to someone's rescue, whether or not that someone realized he or she needed assistance.

Occasionally, Georgia enlisted the help of a friend. Sometimes she sat still long enough—in person or at the other end of a telephone line—to hear advice.

Her latest crisis was clear.

Georgia needed a boy.

Not really a boyfriend, not someone to go steady with,

or to exchange undying vows of affection and purpose. What she needed was a guy to hang out with.

There she was in eighth grade already, all too conscious that other girls around her had suitors and pals and friends of the male persuasion. She didn't.

She began to cast her eyes around hourly, listing the pluses and minuses of each boy she saw in her classes. Some boys—even though Georgia felt just a little guilty—were excluded on the basis of looks alone. She knew that she was probably making mistakes, that unless she made an effort she would never know whether Boy A or Boy B really had a personality that was a match for her own if she were basing everything on physical features alone.

Nonetheless, that was where she started.

At the end of a particularly frenzied day, Georgia called one of her best friends, Charlotte Bracken. This was customary. If the two didn't see one another after school, the minute one got home she dialed the other.

"All right!" Georgia said enthusiastically into her receiver. "I've found him!"

She paused dramatically. Charlotte, having known Georgia since kindergarten, didn't take the bait. She sat with the telephone to *her* ear, silently, waiting. There was no way Georgia could keep a secret.

"David Phillips!"

Georgia couldn't stand more than a few seconds of silence as Charlotte considered her choice. "Well, what about him? Why not? What's wrong with him?"

Charlotte did not take Georgia's questions lightly. She

was a sober girl who took her responsibilities seriously. "He's not in your league, Georgia," she said coolly. "Not today, not tomorrow."

"How can you be so sure?"

"I'm sure of only one thing. He's cute," Charlotte replied. "I'll give you that. He's cute. He's also very, very short."

"He'll grow!" Georgia defended. "His father's as tall as mine!"

"Georgia, there's nothing between his ears," Charlotte explained patiently. "He means well. He likes you, I'm sure. He's sweet. But he's not smart."

"He probably just hasn't found himself," Georgia said rather weakly. "I mean, some people don't find themselves for years and years."

"You want to wait? How long?"

Georgia's eyes closed, resigned. She knew Charlotte was right. Charlotte Bracken seemed—at least nine times out of ten—right about everything: clothes, music, boys, teachers, homework, tests.

Georgia nodded then, admitting defeat. "Well," she decided finally, "I just thought he was . . . you know, interesting."

"It's not the end of the world, Georgia."

Georgia did not even bother to reply. Clearly Charlotte didn't understand the urgency of settling down, settling in, taking one's place among one's peers.

"He is cute," Charlotte said softly. "Maybe I'm wrong."

"No, you're not."

"Keep looking," Charlotte counselled.

"I don't have time to do that! I mean, every other girl in school hangs out with someone. How much longer can it be before people notice and start to talk about me?"

Charlotte laughed just a little. "Georgia, one: I don't hang out. And two: you never in your life cared whether or not people talked about you. In fact, if they didn't, that's when you went crazy."

Georgia frowned. Charlotte was right, again. "Later."

"Later."

The next day's crisis, one about which Georgia read in the daily *Owanka Herald,* would provide her with almost everything she imagined she wanted. And from the first she never imagined she wouldn't win.

Chapter 2

At the end of classes the next day, Georgia decided there was one more feature of Charlotte that was constant. Every time Georgia tried to guess what Charlotte would do or say, she was surprised.

On paper, the two were very similar indeed. Both were new eighth graders at Owanka Junior High, situated in a town of just above twelve thousand, if one included the farm families in the surrounding Iowa county. Both were about five-three, and growing. They weighed in at identical poundages. They liked the same people, the same classes, most of the same music.

But where Georgia was alight with emotion—not necessarily romantic, yet, just wild and wildly seeking—Charlotte was inclined to take a cooler view of life.

Georgia had a moment to think about all this as she sat in the crowded, high-ceilinged hearingroom of the

John Neufeld

Owanka Town Hall. It had been such a struggle to get Charlotte even to consider attending this meeting that what she had first said to Georgia hadn't really registered.

In the whispered moments before Mr. Brady called the meeting to order, Charlotte's objections came through loud and clear in Georgia's mind for the first time.

"Georgia, I just don't think our going will be worth anything," Charlotte had said somberly, having been accosted by Georgia half an hour earlier on the sidewalk outside school.

"Of course it is!" Georgia replied quickly. "We're the kids most affected! It's our lives they're trying to keep so clean, so pure!"

Charlotte nodded. Her dark eyes looked serenely into Georgia's lighter ones, and there was just the slightest hint of a smile on her lips. "We don't vote, Georgia. They can ignore us all they want."

"But it's our presence that makes a difference! We fill up the seats! We let them know how we feel! We put pressure on them!"

Charlotte's grin grew. "Georgia, listen to me. My people have been in this country for hundreds of years. We've filled up the seats. We've let *everyone* know how we feel. We put pressure on the whole country. You really think *we've* made progress?"

"But of course you have!" Georgia defended. "Of course you have!"

Charlotte shook her head. "Georgia, you're on fire *now*. Black people have been on fire *since we got here*. So, if

6

you'll excuse me, I don't think I'll go with you. Taking the long view as I do" —and Charlotte couldn't help smiling at her own words because she knew how much they resembled what her father would have said— "I'll sit this one out."

Georgia's mouth was agape and her blue eyes wider than usual as Charlotte patted her shoulder and walked away, cradling her textbooks against her chest.

But Charlotte had reversed directions once more. For the sake of her friendship with Georgia, she was sitting patiently four rows behind her, waiting to hear which way the wind was about to blow.

Neither girl had any idea that they were in the path of a hurricane.

Chapter 3

Georgia had to sit up straight in order to see over other people's heads and shoulders. She leaned forward, too, the better to hear what Stanley Sopwith was going to say.

She ignored the dark glance shot at her by her older sister, Ava, seated two rows ahead and slightly to the right. It wasn't Georgia's fault if Ava's boyfriend thought she was an honest human being and worth something, too, despite her age.

The hearingroom was packed with other Iowa citizens curious to know just what it was Stanley Sopwith had discovered on his assignment. Apart from a huge American flag behind the dais, the public space on the second floor of Owanka's town hall was unadorned. But it throbbed with emotion and puzzlement.

It seemed to Georgia that many people, like herself,

were holding their breaths. She looked to both sides of where she sat.

She saw a lot of familiar faces. Owanka was a small town. Some she would have expected; some not.

One she did not expect, and had never before seen, sat across the aisle from her on an end chair, a boy who smiled at her as her eyes met his. Georgia was so startled by this she had no time even to blush. She looked away quickly, and then, slyly, tried to look back unobserved.

She didn't know him. She hadn't seen him in the hallway at school. She doubled her fingers into a fist and hit her own knee. Why was Charlotte seated somewhere else? She would have known who this guy was.

He wasn't cute. Cute would have been the wrong word. He was—well, she couldn't find the word, really. Mature-looking came to her mind, but that didn't begin to describe his appeal. He had light brown hair and he wore glasses, pale gold horn–rims that made him look very bright. Also rather mischievous. Georgia couldn't tell how tall he was, or in what grade he might be.

Georgia was nothing if not strong-willed. She forced her attention away from the feeling that her heart was beating rather faster than usual and back to the matter at hand. It wasn't easy, but she did it. She looked forward again, toward the dais, and considered.

Perhaps one half of the crowd around her had read *The Grapes of Wrath* in school. They could remember, they knew.

The other half hadn't even heard of the book. All they

knew was what they read in *The Owanka Herald,* which was that a committee of one—Stanley Sopwith—had been appointed by the chair of the city council, Mr. Fairchild Brady, to report at the next meeting on whether or not the book was un-American, a threat to school-children, prurient, filled with language and images that by rights shouldn't be forced on any student against his or her will.

Georgia thought—although she herself had not yet read the book, since it was assigned reading for the kids two grades ahead of her (maybe *he* was that far ahead of her)—that the people around her who had read the book had obviously survived the experience. They had gradu-ated, gone to college or work, married, had children. Life for these people had not been tainted by their experience.

For the others, Georgia suspected they were unwitting cattle waiting to be herded by Fairchild Brady into a stam-pede. The election was just six weeks away. Mr. Brady was running once again for citywide office. In Georgia's estimation, he had uncovered an issue that would moti-vate his followers to come out to support him.

But even she did not foresee the match that Stanley Sopwith was going to throw so close to her that she would self-combust.

Chapter 4

"I think it might be best," Stanley Sopwith announced in a voice nearly trembling with strange emotions, "if women and whatever young people are in the room leave the hall temporarily until I conclude my report."

No one moved.

"I'm serious," Mr. Sopwith insisted. "This gets pretty rough."

"Stanley?"

Mr. Sopwith looked quickly up at the secretary of the city council, Mrs. Clarke. Mrs. Clarke had been married three times. Each of her husbands had succumbed to sudden disease, swiftly and reportedly without undue pain. Among some people in Owanka, this caused speculation about Mrs. Clarke's talents in the kitchen.

"Really, dear," Mrs. Clarke said sweetly, "I think most of us are adult enough, and discreet enough, to be able to take what you're going to tell us in the spirit in which it is offered. Do, go ahead."

Stanley Sopwith did not look happy. After a few seconds, since no one else seemed to agree with his suggestion, he shrugged. "I myself have not yet concluded reading the book in question," he began. He looked out at his audience, almost challengingly. He dropped the pages he held to his side. "I couldn't!" he announced loudly. "It was too much! I never in my life ran across anything like it!"

Some people in the hearingroom seemed to sigh. Georgia couldn't tell whether the sound she heard was one of relief or of concern.

"Stanley," Fairchild Brady cautioned from the dais, "try to be impartial, if you please."

"That's impossible!" Stanley Sopwith shot back. "Why, if I'd known this book was in our school, I'd have single-handedly raided that place and torn it out, every last copy, book by book, its Pulitzer Prize be damned!"

Chapter 5

Mr. Brady nodded rather sympathetically. "What does your report conclude?" he asked quietly.

Mr. Sopwith calmed himself and once more lifted the sheaf of papers he held. "In my initial perusal," he read carefully, "I found blasphemy, un-Americanism, the espousal of communism and other foreign ideologies, not to mention more examples of obscene language than I had ever before heard or read."

The assembly was spellbound, breathless, waiting.

"In the first one hundred pages," Stanley Sopwith continued at last, after taking a big breath, "this is what I found."

In his left hand he held a crushed piece of Kleenex, with which to wipe his forehead. The room was silent, but for a few people squeaking forward on their chairs.

"Mind you," warned Mr. Sopwith suddenly, "this is only the first one hundred pages!"

Ava Van Buren, on the staff of Owanka High's *The Hawk,* wrote every word as quickly as she could. She had put her annoyance at finding Martin Brady two rows behind her, sitting next to her own sister, Georgia, aside. Temporarily.

"There are twenty uses of the word 'damn.' There are thirty-one instances of the word 'hell.' 'Goddamn' is used fifteen times. 'Jesus' eighteen, 'Christ' seven, and 'son-of-a-bitch' twelve."

Mr. Sopwith paused, triumphant, eyes aglitter. He half-turned toward Fairchild Brady, expecting that he would be asked to proceed no further. But Mr. Brady said nothing, sitting motionlessly, a tiny smile on his lips, coaxing silently.

"What on earth," whispered Georgia Van Buren to Martin, "is he waiting for?"

Martin Brady smiled sideways at her. "These are Stanley's fifteen minutes."

"What does that mean?" Georgia asked.

Martin shook his head, half-raising his hand toward her, urging patience and silence.

"The word 'bastard' is used eight times. Drinking, or being drunk, is mentioned approvingly nine times. God's name is taken twenty-five times!"

A concerned murmur rippled through the crowd.

"He's on a roll now," Martin advised Georgia.

Which must have been what Stanley Sopwith himself was thinking. His voice strengthened and speeded up. He read from his list with increasing anger and mounting pleasure, although he would have been the first to deny this.

"Fornicating with women is mentioned approvingly

eight times, as in 'tom-cattin' and 'layin' with.' Killing, and showing no signs of remorse, killing human beings is mentioned four times, along with an avowed intention to do the same again, guiltlessly. Rape is mentioned twice. The word 'bitch' is used four times. 'Ass' is used three. The lack of differentiation between good and evil, between sin and goodness, is mentioned three times. Euphemisms for the male member are used four times. And the following are mentioned at least once, all in these same one hundred pages: 'breasts,' 'crap,' 'orgasm,' 'cussing,' 'screwing,' 'testicles.' There is one instance of a pig eating a human child! And there is one instance of people actually having sex . . . with animals!!"

The hearingroom was totally silent. Mouths opened silently. Eyes were wide.

Mr. Sopwith was perspiring and weaving just the slightest bit in his place. He was not a big man, or a particularly handsome one. He was widely regarded as wifeless, childless, and humorless, with ears that stuck out so one could almost picture the two-wing construction of the old plane that his name brought to mind. A grain merchant and construction company vice president, his face was usually gray, his figure sparse, his clothing pressed so often that people remarked unkindly they could see their own reflections in the shine of worn gabardine under certain lights whenever Stanley bent over.

"All in all," Mr. Sopwith concluded, "I found two hundred and seventeen instances of what I consider objectionable language, imagery, or ideology. That is more than two instances per page, and certainly more than any book ought rightfully to have in its entirety." He drew his Kleenex across his forehead.

"Thank you, Stanley," Fairchild Brady said comfortingly. "That was quite a task and we're all grateful to you for doing it so well."

"'And for being my lackey,'" Georgia Van Buren muttered to everyone nearby.

Mr. Sopwith barely smiled and looked around, apparently wondering whether he was to resume his seat or remain standing, perhaps half-expecting applause.

Mr. Brady coughed once, gently. Stanley sat down.

Fairchild Brady was a handsome man, dressed in a cleanly pressed white shirt and a pin-striped suit with Oxford shoes, his gray-white hair slicked back and just the slightest bit damp over his red forehead. He brought up his hand to cover his mouth as he coughed politely one more time and cleared his throat. And then he looked out over the crowd.

Only to see a figure on its feet several rows away. A look of annoyance dashed across his face but it was easily camouflaged. "Yes, Martin?"

Fairchild Brady's older son was standing in his place, next to Georgia. "I guess a lot of people, hearing Mr. Sopwith's report, would be shocked," Martin said carefully. "But I have one question for him I'd like answered."

"And what is that?" asked his father calmly.

"Could Mr. Sopwith please tell us what the book is about?"

Chapter 6

Some people, including Georgia, laughed into their chests. Even Ava, seated not far away and trying hard to be objective, because she believed that was the role of "the press," had to smile. Georgia glanced quickly at the boy across the aisle. He, too, smiled.

Mr. Brady looked down at Stanley Sopwith. "Stanley?"

Mr. Sopwith rose once more to his feet. "You mean the story?"

Martin Brady nodded.

Mr. Sopwith reddened. "I could not," he said defiantly. "And I wouldn't, even if I could. It was all I could do to get through one hundred pages of that filth! Who cares what kind of story the man thinks he's telling?"

"Well, sir," Martin said courteously, "I think that may matter to some of us here. You see, I read that book in tenth grade myself. I don't feel sullied by it, or cheapened, or cynical."

"Probably weren't so damned pure to begin with!" Mr. Sopwith said under his breath.

Mr. Brady glared down from above.

"You see, I'm not certain," Martin continued then, "that anyone could have told the same kind of tragic story Mr. Steinbeck did without using most of the words and ideas you find so threatening."

Martin Brady sat down. There was no smirk on his face. He had finished what he had to say.

"You stick to your guns, son!" came an angry shout from the back corner of the hearingroom.

People turned to see a man who looked to be at least ninety standing, red in the face, hand in the air made into a fist.

"Mr. Nagle, I believe?" queried Fairchild Brady.

"You believe right," Mr. Nagle agreed. "I was principal of that school when the book first came out. I taught it in my English classes. I was the one who put it on a reading list for the first time. It's a story we older people know about because we lived it, we saw people broken by it. It's an honest and heartbreaking job, that book, and the language it uses is the language of its time and place."

Mr. Brady nodded placatingly and attempted to cut off Mr. Nagle in midthought. "Then you think the book is suit—"

"Damned right I do!" said Mr. Nagle. "There isn't

another book about the Depression that even begins to touch it. It's American and solid and true. And if a bunch of right-wing ignoramuses try to remove it from the hands of young people who should know about that part of their country's history, well, I for one will go to the wall defending it."

"Now just a minute," Stanley Sopwith said, standing and pointing his finger at Mr. Nagle. A flashbulb erupted.

"If the shoe fits, Sopwith," Mr. Nagle challenged.

"I'm no ignoramus!" shouted Stanley.

"No, you just read a hundred pages of one of America's greatest books without the faintest idea of what the man was saying. That's not ignorance. That's illiteracy!"

"Gentlemen, gentlemen," cautioned Mr. Brady, "there's no need to—"

"Yes, there is too, Fairchild," shouted Nagle. "You've got to call a spade a spade, no matter what. There's more than enough to attend to in this town without meddling in the education of the young."

Georgia noticed that Mrs. Nichols, chairwoman of the school board, which was supposed to be independent to begin with, nodded at this. On the dais she sat just beside the council's treasurer, Mr. Hubbell.

"We are not meddling, Benjamin," Mr. Brady replied. "All we're doing is questioning the good sense of a teacher assigning something to his or her class that we feel is lurid and cheap or pornographic."

"Pornographic!" snorted Mr. Nagle, still on his feet.

"I'll tell you what's pornographic! Censorship, that's what!"

Just at that moment, the photographer from *The Owanka Herald* sprang from his seat and swung around quickly to flash a picture of Mr. Nagle, hand raised, the cords in his neck clear, his eyes huge in outrage.

Chapter 7

"I told you this was going to happen!" Georgia announced to her family that night at dinner.

Georgia's family knew, after thirteen years, that she was a young woman filled with flame. Sometimes, according to her father, Fred, they exploded in tinder-dry countryside, filling the air with ash and smoke so that the lay of the land completely disappeared.

"And you were right," Fred Van Buren soothed. "I admit it. I was wrong not to have seen things as clearly as you."

Georgia stared at her father. This was an unusual admission. Her father generally made light of Georgia's crises, cautioning time after time that the world would move forward at its pace, not hers.

Her mother, more often than not a gentle supporter of her younger daughter's views, smiled the length of the dining table at her husband.

"Pass the gravy," Jonny Van Buren demanded, eleven years of manners forgotten.

"Please," prompted his father.

"Please," echoed Jonny obediently.

"So, what I need to know now is," Georgia explained, trying to ignore her brother's habits, "are you coming with me tomorrow?"

Seeing her father's puzzled look, Ava Van Buren leaned forward slightly in her chair. "Mr. Brady decided to postpone final action until then. The crowd had gotten unruly."

"What I don't understand is what on earth can be wrong with such an ancient book," Georgia wondered.

"I thought Mr. Brady found it un-American and dirty," said her mother. "Or poor Stanley did. As I remember," she added thoughtfully, "it's just a terribly sad story of people during the Depression, fighting to get along, to put food on the table, to get to California where they think life will be better."

"That doesn't sound so awful to me," Georgia allowed.

"You haven't read it?" asked her father.

Georgia shook her curls, looking a little like a Victorian street urchin portrayed by Charles Dickens: straight, sharp nose, brightly colored cheeks, wide blue eyes. "We don't get it until tenth grade. Matt Brady's in tenth grade. That's how his father found it."

"Perhaps his father has a point," Fred Van Buren suggested. "Maybe parts of it are rough."

"Life is rough," Georgia replied quickly, bringing a thin smile to her father's face. "Don't you all see what this could mean?" Georgia raised her voice in disbelief. "Censorship! Dictatorship!"

"In sleepy little Owanka?" teased her father.

Georgia was unconsciously dramatic—part of the time. She sighed hugely and let her hands flap limply to her sides. "What makes you think it couldn't happen here? A man says that he thinks other people shouldn't read a certain book. That man is on the city council. He has influence on the school board. He is running for re-election."

"And so?" encouraged her mother.

"So, what's to keep him from suggesting later that another book is just as bad, that it be removed from school? Or maybe even hundreds of other books? Whole libraries could be destroyed!"

"As I recall, darling," said Alva Van Buren carefully, "that book was written and published for grown-ups. Sometimes—and I don't mean this personally, Georgia, just generally—sometimes we all assume you children are so much more adult and sophisticated than we were at your age that we forget a line does still exist between you and us."

"What on earth does that mean?" Georgia asked.

"What your mother means," explained her father, "is that sometimes adults, teachers, and parents overestimate the capabilities of the young."

"Do I presume," Georgia said, straightening in her

chair and sitting absolutely rigidly, her voice trembling, "that you mean me?"

"If the shoe fits," Jonny slipped in slyly.

"You read it, Ava. What did you think?"

Ava shrugged. "There are some words in it," Ava said rather weakly.

"Like what?" Jonny asked eagerly.

"Never mind." Georgia was impatient. "Go on. What else is in it?"

"The usual stuff," Ava hedged. "A little sex, a little profanity."

"What would make it un-American?" Georgia wanted to know.

"Honestly, I don't know," her sister replied. "I mean, it is about American families, facing American problems. I don't really think it could be un-American."

Georgia thought a moment and, when she spoke, her voice had dropped into a dramatic register. "This is how it starts," she intoned. "No one feels really threatened at first. After all, we can read about this in the newspaper, so we still have a free press. At first nothing seems to affect us personally, so we ignore it. We smile a little. Then, suddenly, one day you wake up and it's too late! We're slaves!"

"Sweetheart," Alva Van Buren interjected, "what are you reading now?"

Georgia reddened.

"Well?" Her mother waited.

"The Diary of Anne Frank."

Fred Van Buren's mouth twitched to repress his smile and Alva averted her eyes.

"Well, for heaven's sakes," Ava decided. "That explains the whole thing!"

"It most certainly does not!" Georgia was firm.

"Of course it does," Ava said. "You're all nerve ends from that, looking for oppression and disaster everywhere."

"What none of you seems to realize," Georgia announced with sudden dignity, standing at her place, "is that Anne Frank aside, the kind of thing that happened years ago in Europe can happen anywhere, anytime, unless we're all determined to stand up for our rights."

"Don't forget to take something with you, dear," suggested Georgia's mother, motioning around the table so that Georgia would take a plate or two at the same time she stalked dramatically out of the room.

Chapter 8

"Yes, I am, but don't expect me to be her."

That was what Georgia said every fall to her teachers when she entered a new grade.

Yes, she was Ava Van Buren's younger sister. And no, she was not much like her, so back off.

There was little competition between the two. There were almost four years between them in age, and generally Ava adopted the pose of a knowing and almost sympathetic acquaintance.

Ava was a senior at Owanka High. She was dark-haired, and while her eyes were almost the same color as Georgia's, her face was more angular. She had a broad forehead of which she was proud because someone had once told her that this was a sign of intelligence.

While Georgia dashed in and out of emergencies, Ava was more deliberate. She had a tendency to think ahead, rather than to let her emotions rule. She knew, for example, that extracurricular activities were important to colleges. She was now president of the school's synchronized swimming team, the Sharks, state champions, after putting in three hard years earlier. She had been on the student council for four years running. She was a soloist in her church choir. She held a part-time job on Saturdays at *Chez Elle,* a boutique on the city square.

She was also a reporter on the Owanka High *Hawk.* She had been disappointed not to be chosen its editor, but she swallowed her feelings and stayed aboard. She enjoyed the work. She knew it would be another reason she might be more desirable as a college entrant than others with equal grades.

After nine that evening, Ava was studying French. She had chosen French not because she particularly liked France and all things French, but because it was harder to master than Spanish. Mr. Einaudi, who taught both languages, had made this clear. But she imagined that her intellectual efforts would help her stand out in a crowd of eager would-be freshmen.

She invented another reason that she thought would impress during a college interview: she hoped, she would say, to go to Africa after college and to do work there that would be helpful to the natives. Many of the countries of western Africa had been French colonies, and she would need to be able to speak and read and understand if she were to be worth the price of passage.

Actually, when Ava rehearsed this mentally, she wasn't at all certain that this wasn't really a good plan.

When Georgia edged her way rather timidly into Ava's room, Ava was struggling with irregular verb forms.

"Ava?"

Ava did not look up. She nodded a little, to acknowledge her sister, but kept repeating in her mind the words on the page.

"Will you do me a favor?"

"What?"

"Will you?"

"I don't work that way," Ava said evenly. "You know that."

Georgia eased down onto Ava's bed and stretched out on her stomach, her hands holding up her head. "Will you come to the meeting with me tomorrow?"

Ava turned around to look at her sister. "You don't really need me," she said kindly.

"I didn't say I needed you. I said I wanted you. Of course, since you're on *The Hawk,* you ought to go anyway."

"*The Herald* will cover it."

"So why'd you go today?"

Ava shrugged. "It seemed something I should do. It was sort of fun."

"Fun?" Georgia was appalled.

"Georgia, look. The worst thing that happens is the book is removed from our reading lists. Who cares? You can buy a copy of it somewhere else, at a drugstore or a bookstore if it's so important to you."

"That would make me feel sleazy. Why should I have to sneak around if it's harmless?"

"That's what your meeting tomorrow will determine, won't it? Whether or not it's harmless."

"No," Georgia answered quickly. "What tomorrow will tell us is whether the town will have to vote to remove it or not. I mean, what is this about?

"Censorship. I agree with you."

Georgia sat up. "You have a duty," she advised. "You could skip just one practice. Say you have a dentist appointment or something."

"I told you *The Herald* will be there. Everyone can read about it the next morning. We only come out once a week."

"You don't think the school should have something to say about all this? What about our teachers?"

"What about them?"

"Well, if this idea gets on a ballot and actually passes, suddenly they'll be working for everyone in town."

"They do now," Ava said.

"You know what I mean. They're supposed to be experts. They train and get degrees."

"So?"

"The school board hires them to do the best they can for us, with all their experience behind them. How can they do that if this passes?"

"You have a point, I suppose."

"You have to rally us, Ava. You can do it. You can write about everything so that the teachers know we support them, their work. That we appreciate what they do."

Ava frowned thoughtfully. "That would be slanting the news, Georgia. That isn't what I would do."

"Even Peter Jennings lets us know how he feels about things, without words, you know what I mean?"

"Yes, I suppose I do."

"Ava?"

"What?"

"Do you like muscles on boys?"

Ava laughed, but kindly. "Yes, I rather do."

"You like the way boys all hang out together lifting weights? The way they swagger around, all pumped up?"

"Well, not that, so much."

Georgia was pleased. The boy who had been at the meeting seemed to have been normal-looking, too.

"Do you think it makes them more attractive?"

"No, not really."

"Then what?"

Ava smiled again, this time more to herself than to her sister, thinking of Martin Brady. "Well, their arms feel good when they're around you."

Chapter 9

"But you must come!" Georgia insisted, standing outside school with Charlotte Bracken.

"I can't, Georgia, I told you. I have my piano lesson."

"What's one lesson in the face of totalitarianism?"

Charlotte laughed.

"Well, there's another reason, then," Georgia admitted slowly. "You weren't home last night so I couldn't tell you."

Charlotte held her books close to her chest and waited.

"There's a boy," Georgia said.

Charlotte said nothing.

"Don't you care?" Georgia nearly shrieked.

"I know there's a boy, Georgia. There are always boys. What boy are we talking about?"

"That's just it. I don't know."

Charlotte sighed dramatically nearly as often as Georgia did.

"He was at the meeting yesterday. He has light brown hair and he wears glasses. And he smiled at me. I lost him in the crowd later, which is probably just as well because I wouldn't have known what to say to him, anyway."

"*He* might have said something. Boys talk from time to time."

"Thank you for that information," Georgia replied. "The point I'm making is that you have to come with me in case he's there again. You'll know who he is!"

"One, I told you I can't. Two, I don't know everyone in school, Georgia, really. You just think I do."

"But they all—"

Charlotte raised her hand to stop her friend. "Think a minute, Georgia. You were going to say that everyone knows me. That isn't true, either. They know I'm black. There are six other Afro-American kids in school, too. Naturally we stand out."

Georgia had to admit this was probably true. She nodded. "Still and all, I need your help. As a friend."

Charlotte grinned. "You'll have it, I promise. Just not this afternoon."

"But what if he shows up again?"

"Then go for it, Georgia. That's easy, isn't it? I mean, you already have something in common."

"What?" Georgia asked eagerly.

"You both like to attend big meetings."

Chapter 10

The first settlers of Owanka had an eye for natural beauty. A freshwater pond was discovered and Owanka built on its banks. On the east side of the pond was an old-fashioned town square, surrounded by brick buildings three stories tall, some of which had white Colonial columns on their porches.

There were still shingles, hung out by doctors and attorneys, on fence posts and lamppoles. There was a department store on the north side of the square (Younkers). City Drug stood to one side of this and *Chez Elle,* the tiny boutique where Ava worked on Saturdays, stood on the other.

Along the west side of the square was a park that led down to the banks of the pond, with benches and shuffleboard courts, and a playground with slides, jungle gym, swings and sandpiles.

Like other small towns, Owanka experienced little high life in its downtown. East of the city by two miles lay a new shopping mall with a sports shop, a record and card store, twin cinemas, a Sears, a discount drug, a pizza joint, a Sizzler's Steakhouse, a supermarket, and a bookstore. Because Owanka High was halfway between the city center and this shining new paradise, that was where its kids hung out.

On the square's south side was the town hall, a multipurpose building that included the courthouse, the local jail, a Department of Motor Vehicles office, a game warden's office. The building itself was impressive: columns freshly painted each spring running to their full three stories, and an imposing bank of stairs leading up to its double doors.

At the top of the steps was a statue, greening and bird-splattered, of Owanka's Civil War hero, Major General Leonard Carl Padway. Despite being on the run at Gettysburg, leading his men to scatter and hide in the Pennsylvania countryside, the legendary major general was forced into somehow holding, single-handedly, a bumpy, insignificant but, after more than a hundred years, an immortal ridge against the CSA rebels.

Fairchild Brady—who secretly thought that in the future, perhaps after his death, a second statue would be placed at the top of the city hall's steps depicting *him*— was once more on the dais at the front of the hearingroom, smiling and nodding and waving discreetly to his friends and followers as they filled the room. The late afternoon light slanted above the crowd.

The meeting did not begin promptly. People shuffled in slowly, looked at the dais to see who was there, greeted neighbors and friends, settled in noisily. Owanka's one trial lawyer sat a few chairs away from Ava, who had fabricated an excuse to attend after all. The photographer from *The Herald* was in a front-row seat, loading his camera, checking his equipment and flash attachment.

Georgia sat between two women whose faces were not widely recognized: a reporter from *The Herald* named Susan Woods, and Owanka's junior and senior high school librarian, Laura McCandless.

Georgia looked around to see whether Mr. Nagle, the ancient firebrand of the day before, had made it. She did not see him.

Actually, looking for Mr. Nagle was just a way she could guiltlessly scan the room for the boy from the day before. She craned and twisted. She didn't see him.

At last Mr. Brady raised his gavel and brought the meeting to order. Mrs. Clarke, she of the doubtful culinary skills, was directed to read the minutes from yesterday's set-to. The simple recounting of what had occurred and of what Stanley Sopwith had reported stirred the crowd, and it seemed clear that the people who had come to this second meeting had stronger and louder ideas to express than before.

"Ladies and gentlemen, please," called Fairchild Brady, both of his hands spread wide at shoulder height pacifically. "Please."

After a few more seconds the room began to quiet

John Neufeld

down. Mr. Brady was gratified. "We're here this afternoon, cooler heads and calmer hearts—I hope—" No
one laughed. He coughed self-importantly and resumed.

"What we need to decide today is whether or not *The
Grapes of Wrath* is a book we want our schoolchildren to
have at their beck and call. We would be printing a special
ballot, to accompany the state ballot for this November,
on which we would be asked to declare our feelings."

Mrs. Nichols, of the school board, rose from her chair
behind Mr. Brady. "Are you saying, Fairchild, that the
vote would be binding, or advisory only?"

"I should think binding, wouldn't you?" replied Mr.
Brady smoothly.

"Not if you intend to have a school board in this
town," Mrs. Nichols said firmly.

Mr. Brady opened his eyes wide and spread his hands
palm up. "Are you planning to resign, Louise?"

"My plans are my plans, Fairchild. I'm only warning
you. We have had a long history here of unanimity in our
attitudes toward our children's education. Your two children have benefitted from this.

"Until now, we have seldom had arguments about
taxes or salaries. Parents have been glad to work cooper-
atively with us and our teachers, and they have—until
now—seemed to agree that the best teachers of children
are teachers, professionally hired and trained. I see no
reason to alter this in any way."

Stanley Sopwith leapt to his feet. "Well, I do!" he
shouted up at Mrs. Nichols, a woman of forty-five,

mother of four, trim and neat and generous to her community beyond her position on the school board. "After what I found in that book, it's clear as day to me that your so-called professionals are nothing more than frustrated child molesters!"

The hearingroom erupted with disagreement. Mr. Brady tried to calm Stanley Sopwith at the same time he smiled encouragingly out at the crowd.

Ava leaned forward to see a faintly familiar figure stand and raise her hand, waiting motionlessly until she was recognized by Mr. Brady. "Yes, ma'am?" he said over the remaining murmur of argument.

"Without taking sides on this issue, I'd like to introduce myself," said the woman clearly and evenly. She was in her early thirties, tall and nicely proportioned, wearing a gray flannel suit and simple blouse, her dark brown hair hanging free.

Ava wrote frantically.

"I am the librarian at Owanka junior and senior high schools and my name is Laura McCandless. It might be helpful, whether or not you eventually put this issue before the voters, for you to know that at the library we have forms that can be used to make these matters a little clearer."

She picked up her purse and walked toward the front of the large room. She was also carrying a sheaf of official-looking printed white paper. She handed one page each of these to Mr. Brady and to Mrs. Nichols.

"I brought these along," Ms. McCandless explained,

"because from time to time other complaints are made about particular books in our collections, and these help to identify not just the books, but the precise reasons why someone feels they are unsuitable for young people."

Mr. Brady glanced quickly at the page in his hand. Then he smiled too easily and his voice sounded a little patronizing. "I can see how helpful these might be in another case. But in this instance, we have already identified the book and the reasons we think it unworthy of our younger citizens' time and attention."

Without meaning to, Georgia snorted. The noise wasn't gigantic but it was audible.

"I'm not certain I agree, Fairchild," Mrs. Nichols announced. "Really, I think this is a very sensible idea."

"I don't doubt that, Louise," Mr. Brady assured her. "But it seems to me that later, perhaps in other instances, once we've taken care of this book, we can—"

"No, I think this is the perfect time," Mrs. Nichols persisted. "Think. If Stanley had filled out one of these, the school board would have had a record of his complaint and we could have acted on it without going to all the trouble and expense and clearly the unpleasantness of a public hearing. That, after all, is what the school board is for, Fairchild."

Mr. Brady seemed uncertain for once what to say next. Mrs. Nichols took another firm step into the silence.

"I would imagine that whenever we received one of these, from whomever it might be and about whatever book, we would examine the book ourselves and come to a reasonable conclusion about its merits and value. Really, Fairchild, our responsibility is to the young people of Owanka, not to the adults around them."

"And just what about the adults?" Stanley Sopwith asked angrily. "Shouldn't we, based on our experiences of the world, be able to make some of those decisions that help young people get on in the world?"

"Of course you should, Stanley," said Mrs. Nichols logically, gently. "And you are especially free to do so with your own children."

Georgia smothered her laugh. Cool! Old Stanley had no kids. Her amusement was shared by others in the room, equally discreetly.

"What *is* on that piece of paper?" asked the oft-widowed Mrs. Clarke.

Mr. Brady spoke to the entire room. "There are simple questions. She wants to know the name of the book and its author. The reason one might find it objectionable. What the book is about. What other book one would recommend that covers the same subject that is more suitable. Whether one read all the book, parts of it, scanned it, heard about it. What grades your children are in."

"Well," said Mrs. Clarke, leaning back in her chair, her bosom bouncing ever so slightly, "I think that all sounds perfectly reasonable. Why *don't* we let the school board deal with this?"

"Because they'll duck it!" Stanley Sopwith said hotly.

"We go with this kind of thing, it's the last we'll ever hear."

"I take exception to that, *Mister* Sopwith," said Mrs. Nichols with some annoyance. "What this would institute is a channel for complaints and a system for dealing with them."

"This is not the future," Mr. Brady said rather angrily. "Mr. Sopwith was directed to give his recommendations, not his literary opinion. The only question left is whether we feel strongly enough to put the issue to our fellow townspeople."

Mrs. Nichols was not satisfied. "But surely, now that Ms. McCandless has brought us this . . . I mean, you can see how heated people get, how angry. Surely this would be a perfect way of examining and weighing the merits of a book without making people purple in the face."

"For the *future!*" Mr. Brady declared. "Here and now we have a book that requires our attention."

"Vote!" cried Amos Allen suddenly and gruffly. While the room heard him speak, he seemed not to have breathed. A widower, glum and drear, Amos Allen lived on a farm just beyond the city's limits, although thirty acres of his land was incorporated. He worked and farmed alone, making a comfortable living from cattle, hogs, and soybeans. People in Owanka recalled that he and his wife had a son, but no one could remember ever meeting him.

Where Fairchild Brady was rotund, Amos Allen was narrow. His skin was weathered-white, summer and winter, from always wearing a hat, and his hair beneath it was full and dark.

"I second the motion!" Stanley Sopwith declared next, even though he wasn't a member of the council.

Mr. Brady grabbed the moment, disregarding *Robert's Rules of Order.* "The motion is called. Should a separate ballot be printed and distributed along with the regular, this one asking whether people think the book *The Grapes of Wrath* should be removed from the curriculum of the tenth grade at Owanka High, and from the library there?"

"The library?" Ms. McCandless was heard to gasp.

"Might as well." Stanley Sopwith glared at her.

"Now, folks," Mr. Brady said, reclaiming his preelection megaphone, "you've heard the question put. Let's vote."

"Who's going to pay for the ballots?" asked Mr. Allen glumly, his mouth barely moving.

"Well, Amos, I imagine we can find a little extra money in the budget somehow," Mr. Brady reassured. "We're not talking about thousands of dollars, are we? Probably only fifty or sixty bucks all tolled."

Mr. Allen nodded, apparently satisfied.

"Now then," Mr. Brady continued, "all in favor of the motion?"

Georgia, Ava, Ms. McCandless, and everyone else in the hearingroom took no breath.

Mr. Brady's hand raised up toward the ceiling instantly. Mrs. Clarke, long used to being married to *someone* and to giving way, lifted her own.

Mr. Hubbell, treasurer for the council, who usually

kept what was called a low profile, seemed unwilling for a moment to be the center of attention. Then, after a long, thoughtful pause, he opened his mouth. "I abstain."

Mrs. Nichols sat without moving, her hands clasped together in her lap.

Amos Allen twitched. "We shouldn't be getting involved in this," he said almost under his breath. Then, surprising everyone, he raised his hand toward the sky as well.

Mr. Brady smiled as broadly as a proud parent. "Well, then, I guess the motion is carried."

There was a moment of silence in the room, as people inhaled, getting ready to speak for or against what had happened. But before anyone could exhale and begin to orate, from the back of the room came a defiant call. "Fairchild Brady!"

The townspeople swung around in their chairs. Benjamin Nagle was standing just inside the double doors, his face flushed.

"Do you have some new piece of business, Mr. Nagle?" asked Mr. Brady calmly.

"I surely do!" Mr. Nagle said positively. "If you think you can ramrod that book into a cannon and shoot it out of existence, you're dead wrong! You've got a fight on your hands!"

"The electorate will decide," Mr. Brady instructed. "When all is said and done, surely that's the best way to handle things in a democracy like ours."

"I'm not so all-fired sure that your kind of democracy

is like mine!" Nagle shouted back, turning then and pushing back out through the doorway.

"Well, we'll see, won't we?" Mr. Brady called after him.

"You're damned right we'll see!" Mr. Nagle's voice seemed to spring from the emptiness of the hallway, echoing back around the room.

Chapter 11

The meeting had not been long enough for Ava to miss her entire Sharks practice. If she hurried, she might make its last half hour and still have a little time to think about her article for *The Hawk,* describing what had just taken place.

She bent to pick up her purse and her schoolbooks and then stood, craning to see over the crowd, looking for Georgia. She needn't have scoured the faces of her friends and neighbors so diligently. Georgia found her.

"There's a meeting, Ava!" she announced, her face full of excitement.

"Another one?"

"No, a *new* one. For people who want to fight this battle. Come on!"

Ava did not move. "Georgia, I have to get back to school. I can't just get on a runaway train and not look back. I have responsibilities."

Georgia was not impressed. "You have to come, Ava! How can you write the whole thing if you only know a little about it? How can you be impartial if you haven't got all the facts?"

The two began to edge their ways through the standing crowds, overhearing bits and snippets of opinions offered, some quietly, others full of heat.

"Who's running this meeting?" Ava asked as she and Georgia passed through the double doors of the building and stood a moment on the top steps of the town hall.

"Mr. Donald Arrand," Georgia announced grandly, waiting to see the expression on her sister's face.

"The president of the bank?"

Georgia was *very* pleased by Ava's look. "The man himself. I mean, if we needed someone to lead us against Mr. Brady, we couldn't have hoped for more, or better."

Ava stood a moment in thought. Maybe she should go to the meeting, after all.

A beeping from a clean, shiny but ten-year-old pickup parked not far from the bottom of the staircase made both girls turn. The truck was familiar, as was its driver as he leaned across his front seat and opened the passenger door, waiting.

"Oh, good!" Georgia said, starting to run down the steps. "Martin can drop me off!"

Georgia bounded into the truck. Ava followed with more dignity, closing the door after herself.

"Martin, you missed the best meeting!" Georgia began. "And it's just the beginning. Wait 'til I tell you!"

Martin smiled nicely and put the truck into gear, pulling slowly into traffic.

"We're forming a committee, Martin, to fight your father!"

Martin couldn't help laughing quietly. "Good luck," he said sweetly. "My old man doesn't like to lose, at anything."

"Well, he's going to!" Georgia crowed. "I bet everyone who voted on his side is going to lose his council seat!"

Martin looked questioningly across Georgia toward Ava. "You think so, too?" he asked.

Ava shrugged. "You could drop me at school, if you would," she dodged. "I have to get back to practice."

"And you can take me to Mr. Arrand's house, please," Georgia inserted.

"What for?" asked Martin innocently.

"Because *he's* the chairman of our new committee."

"Really?" Martin was both doubtful and, in spite of himself, a little impressed.

"Wait!" Georgia shouted suddenly. "Wait! You can drop me here! I can walk the rest of the way!"

Martin dutifully brought his truck to curbside. Georgia scooted out of the car, across Ava's folded knees. "Thanks, Martin," she called as she turned quickly and started up a tree-lined street toward the top of Owanka's only hill. "When you're ready for a younger woman, you know where to find me!"

Martin laughed.

"She drives me crazy!" Ava said.

"She's a kid," Martin soothed.

The two rode a few moments in silence. Then Ava turned and looked a long minute at Martin Brady. "How do you feel about all this?" she asked quietly.

Martin shook his head. "I don't know. Instinctively more like Georgia than my father. But he is my father."

Ava shrugged, not really hearing the doubt in Martin's voice. "Maybe I'm trying to be too even-handed, too objective. After all, I'm a reporter. That's my role."

"You're a citizen, Ava. That's your real role."

Ava shook her head. "I'm a member of the working press. We don't take sides. We report, purely and simply. Period."

She paused a moment. "You know, this thing could be just the tip of an iceberg. What happens next? Does the school board, or your father, make up a list of forbidden books? I mean, suppose certain words show up in one. Does that mean it's excluded instantly, regardless of how good or bad a book it is? Who has the power?"

"Right now, my old man."

"True, for the time being. But this could set a precedent. The problem is that what your father really wants is to keep his council seat. He's determined. Anything that will help him do that is fair. But if enough people get together to fight him—like Georgia's committee—who knows what will happen?"

"Are you going to enlist?" Martin asked, unable to keep a little surprise from his voice.

Ava looked quickly at him. "I might. I just might."

Chapter 12

"Georgia, come right in."

Donald Arrand took a step backward and motioned Georgia across his threshold. He was a man of sixty, portly, with a circle of white hair that made him seem the image of December. And while he was never heard to laugh "ho-ho-ho!", it was what one might reasonably have expected: the light in his eye, his eagerness to listen, his desire to help.

Georgia was just a little nervous. She knew that people she recognized would be found in the living-room of Mr. Arrand's house. She also suspected there would be people there who surprised her by their very presence.

And she was, after all, compared to the rest of what she imagined Mr. Arrand's friends and neighbors were, very young.

A Small Civil War

"You know a lot of these people, I'm sure," Mr. Arrand said pleasantly as he motioned for her to precede him into the room.

Georgia saw Ms. McCandless, Mr. Nagle, Mrs. Nichols. There were another dozen or so whom she knew she had seen around Owanka although she could not have repeated their names.

Mr. Arrand introduced her to his new cohorts, and then, finally, to a figure who backed into the room carrying a large tray on which were soft drinks, coffee, cups and saucers.

Him!

"And this is my nephew, Constantine."

Georgia was so taken unawares that she didn't even think to wonder at the boy's name. She nodded and added a little smile, looking quickly away to hide her confusion. And delight.

Chapter 13

The meeting had lasted more than an hour, and evening was beginning to drop on the verdant oasis of Owanka, set so pleasingly amid fields and along the pond.

Georgia was being escorted home by Constantine. She had lost her shyness. During the meeting, eventually she had been able to be herself again—outspoken, emotional, positive.

Constantine had been attentive during the session, listening more than contributing. He nodded when he agreed. He never spoke. Every so often he would catch Georgia's eye and they would exchange increasingly frank looks, some serious, some secretively amused.

"But where are your parents?" Georgia wanted to know now as they walked slowly along the sidewalk in the direction of her home.

"In North Africa," Constantine told her.

"But that would be wonderful!" Georgia said. "Can you imagine being there with Berbers and bazaars and camels and sand, miles and miles of sand?"

Constantine smiled easily. "And also terrorists and assassins and disease. That's why I'm here with Uncle Don. My dad was just sent to a new posting. If there's anything serious he's not sure of, he parks me somewhere until the coast is clear. Or at least until he and Mom can arrange things the way they want them and feel good about having me around."

"But don't you miss them?"

"Sure," Constantine agreed. "But it's nice here, too."

Georgia shook her head. Given a choice, she would take the perils of Morocco or even Libya anytime. She looked over at Constantine. The fading sunlight reflected back into her eyes from his glasses. She wouldn't really be able to see if he were annoyed or not. "Your name," she began. "I mean, it's unusual, for an American."

Constantine smiled to himself. "Not really, when you consider my middle name."

"Which is?"

"Paris."

"Paris? You mean, as in France?" Georgia heard herself and tried suddenly to be more sophisticated. "Of course, maybe it's the man who stole Helen, before the Trojan War."

"No," said her companion. "It's France. You were right the first time."

Georgia nodded and looked down at her feet as she walked.

"There's a story, of course," Constantine said then.

"What?"

Constantine shrugged. "It's simple. I was conceived in Paris, and born in Turkey. Constantine is for Constantinople. My sister got saddled with even worse names."

"What? How old is she? Where is she?"

Constantine put both hands in his pockets. "She's married now. She lives in New York." He paused. "Florence," he said after a second. "Florence Oran." He laughed.

"I don't get it," Georgia admitted.

"Conceived in Oran, which is in Algeria. Years ago, when my dad was posted there. And Florence is Italy, where she was born, when he and Mom were on holiday."

"Florence Oran Arrand," Georgia said slowly. "That's not easy, is it?"

Constantine shook his head.

"But why aren't you in New York with her?"

"Because she and her husband have only a one-bedroom flat," Constantine replied. "Apartment," he modified. "Georgia?"

"Yes?"

"You can call me Con. Not Connie. Never Connie. Some people do and it drives me crazy. But I like Con."

"But isn't that sort of Irish?"

"Sort of," Con agreed. "Half our family is Irish, so really it fits."

Georgia nodded, trying out "Con" in her mind. "What's the other half?"

"Owankan," Con laughed. "My great-grandparents farmed here and started the bank more than a hundred and twenty years ago."

Georgia nodded again. Charlotte Bracken was going to be blown away.

Chapter 14

"But I'm not asking for all that much!" Georgia said sullenly to her father at dinner that night. "All I want to be able to do is pull my own weight. I mean, that's what you've always told us we had to do."

Her father nodded seriously. "I still believe that," he said. "But I also believe that if you're going to get so involved in this, it will mean more, much more to you, if you have to raise your own funds."

"What about your savings account?" asked Georgia's mother.

"How do you think the rich get richer?" Jonny asked quickly with a sudden broad smile.

"Oh, for heaven's sakes!" Georgia said in exasperation.

"Don't you have that much saved up?" Ava asked.

Georgia blushed. "Sure, I guess," she admitted. "But that's supposed to be for college."

"See?" Jonny crowed and started to laugh.

"This isn't funny!" Georgia complained. "Look at it this way. I'd be the representative of the Van Buren family. I mean, suppose everyone chipped in! I'm certainly not proud."

"Who else is involved?" asked her mother then. "This all seems to be happening so quickly."

"Well," Georgia said, hopeful and calmer, "there's me. And Ms. McCandless, although her participation's supposed to be secret, undercover, if you know what I mean. And Mr. Nagle, who used to teach English and was actually principal years and years ago. And there's Mrs. Nichols. Oh, and Mr. Barton, who lives around the corner. He's your friend, Dad. You go fishing in Canada with him."

Georgia's father nodded, apparently unsurprised that one of his own friends was among Georgia's and Don Arrand's committee.

"Is that all?" Ava asked.

"No, those are just the names of people you'd recognize," Georgia answered.

"There's Mrs. Rasmussen, from out at the farm," added Georgia's mother.

"Alva," said her husband, "I thought this was all news to you."

"It was," Mrs. Van Buren nodded. "But it seems Georgia's committee is sweeping the countryside. She called me just before Ava got home."

Fred Van Buren's eyebrows raised slightly. "Anyone else we know?"

"Reverend Fickett," answered his wife.

"Really?" Georgia's father sounded surprised. Then he brightened a bit. "Well, there you are, Georgia girl. Go get Mr. Fickett to give you a loan. Maybe his church will advance you your dues."

"You're not getting the point," Georgia objected. "I'm trying to put my money where my mouth is, not someone else's."

"Then you do that on your own, sweetheart," counseled her father gently. "It will make you feel better for having sacrificed something in order to further your beliefs."

"Something in which *I* believe?" Georgia was suddenly wide-eyed.

"Other people may not feel as strongly as you do, Georgia," said her father, "or agree with you."

"Are you saying you're on the other side?" Georgia demanded.

"No, I'm not saying that," said her father. "All I'm saying is that I'm thinking about this, too, diligently. I've even started rereading the book."

"You have?" asked Georgia's mother.

Fred Van Buren nodded.

"And?" Ava prompted.

"Well, one thing. There *is* an awful lot of rough language involved."

"There's a lot of that in the world," Ava reminded.

"I know," agreed her father. "But I'll tell you something. I'm not at all certain I don't agree with Fairchild Brady.

Our country seems to be going downhill pretty darned fast. Our morals aren't what they were. The crime rate is up. People are dissatisfied, too impatient to work hard for their just rewards, so they picket and burn and loot. Towns like ours are the backbone of this country, after all. Maybe if we straightened ours up a little, stood taller, made a stand, maybe we could actually begin to turn things around."

"Very slowly," Ava guessed.

"Admittedly," her father said. "But also, I think, proudly."

"Fred, I'm absolutely amazed at you," said Mrs. Van Buren.

"No reason to be, Alva," he returned. "I said I hadn't made up my mind. I'm just leaning."

"My own father!" Georgia wailed suddenly, putting her head in her hands dramatically and moaning. "I mean, I haven't read the book yet, but I certainly know I do not like being told whether or not I can. That it's bad for me somehow. I think that decision is strictly up to me!"

"Well," her father said slowly, "not entirely, sweetheart. What are parents for, after all?"

"To give comfort and aid and support!" Georgia shot back.

Fred Van Buren laughed softly. "And also to see that our loved ones are cared for and treated humanely and kept from harm."

"A book is not harmful!" Georgia shrieked.

"*This* book might be," argued her father without raising his voice. "The question is, can this story be told without using those words? I rather think it can. Even that perhaps it should have been."

"But Fred, you're asking an artist to conform to *your* rules," Mrs. Van Buren pointed out. "You wouldn't tell a painter what colors to use, or what style would please *you* most."

"No, I wouldn't," Georgia's father defended logically. "But I might not buy the picture for my own home if I didn't like what was in it."

"But surely," Alva Van Buren persisted, "you wouldn't keep someone else from buying it and hanging it in his home?"

"No, of course not," he agreed.

"Well, there you are!" Georgia crowed triumphantly.

"Shhh!" Ava hissed at her. "Let Mother say that."

If Georgia hadn't spoken—if her mother had been allowed the time to speak—the Van Burens might have meshed and settled and then, later, when important moments came, stood firm.

But that didn't happen.

Chapter 15

Charlotte Bracken's mother had dropped off half a dozen kids at the mall outside Owanka after school's close on Friday. She was to pick them up two hours later.

Con Arrand was old enough to have applied for and been granted a learner's driver's license, but there were two obstacles: one, according to his uncle, it was doubtful whether the Department of Motor Vehicles would grant him the permit since he hadn't a permanent address in the state; secondly, this sort of permit required an adult in the car at all times. Mr. Arrand was a busy man.

Charlotte, Georgia, Con Arrand, Bobby "Legs" Fickett, and two others roamed the high-ceilinged atria, wandering in and out of stores and food shops, eventually using whatever money they had between them to put salsa on any edible surface. They were grateful for water fountains spaced throughout the halls.

Temptations called alluringly from clothing stores and sports-shoe outlets. Music sailed out at them as they passed the record store, and Bobby Fickett and Charlotte bounced into an impromptu dance, gyrating and spinning on the tiled floors for a few minutes until a crowd began to gather. Bobby would have continued but Charlotte came to her senses and became embarrassed.

As the light outside began to fade, and some of the crowds within started to seep into the dusk, Georgia and her friends floated slowly toward an exit where they were to wait for Mrs. Bracken.

"I wish we had places like this," Con said to Georgia as they walked slowly, trailing the others by twenty feet or so.

"Where?"

Con shrugged. "Anywhere," he explained. "I mean, where my folks are usually assigned there are always open markets, filled with stalls and stands, selling stuff. But not like here. All I ever see is fake ruins and antiquities, cloth, fruit and fish that not only smells suspicious, it *looks* suspicious."

"I think that sounds so romantic," Georgia exclaimed. "I'd give anything to be able to travel as you do."

Con nodded. "Yeah," he agreed. "I know I sound ungrateful, but sometimes you just need to be able to call somewhere home. I mean, you don't necessarily have to *be* there all the time, but it sure makes you feel better knowing that there is somewhere you feel is your own, where you can let down, you know, and just hang out and relax."

"Don't you get any feeling like that here?" Georgia asked.

Con blushed. He smiled a little and then slipped his arm over Georgia's shoulder. "I could, maybe." He exerted just enough pressure to make Georgia smile.

"Hey, Con!" Bobby Fickett had turned around and seen the couple. "You two want to be alone?"

"Ignore him," Georgia advised.

"Hey, guys!" Bobby called to his friends. "We've got true love blooming here!"

Georgia blushed.

"Why does he care?" asked Con. "Do you and he have a history?"

Georgia stopped in her tracks. "A history? We're not old enough to have a history. Certainly not."

"Then what's his trouble?"

Georgia smiled and slipped out from under Con's arm. "I don't know. Maybe he's just teasing you because you're new and *you* don't have a history."

"God, I wish I were going to be here next spring," Con said suddenly, almost a little angrily. "I keep hearing how fast Bobby Fickett is in track. I'd really like to whip his butt!"

Georgia laughed. "How do you say that in . . . in whatever language they speak in North Africa?"

Con shrugged.

"The thing is, Con, hanging out is kind of . . . well, just what it sounds like. I mean, when two people—not us, necessarily, just any two people—I mean, they just don't do things alone."

"I don't get it."

Georgia began to think she should have kept her mouth shut. "Well, it's not that there are any rules, not hard and fast ones, anyway. I mean, probably when our folks were kids, they went steady or something. I don't know why exactly, but that kind of thing, really dating someone in particular, isn't anything we do yet."

"We're supposed to be satisfied with proximity?"

"What?"

"Just being within six feet is supposed to mean something?"

Georgia smiled sweetly and reached out to take Con's hand. "I guess so," she admitted.

"Who made those rules?" Con asked, not meaning to be answered. "I mean, what about relationships?"

"Relationships?" Georgia echoed, sounding even to herself astonished.

"Sure," Con said. "Isn't that what we're building here?"

Georgia didn't know what to say. For a minute, she didn't even know how to *look*. She hadn't ever really thought about Con and herself in a *relationship*.

Now that she did, she wasn't displeased. Nervous, maybe, but not unhappy.

Con squeezed Georgia's hand. "You colonials," he said with a laugh as they walked through the doors into the dusk.

"Hey, Con!" Bobby Fickett again.

Con and Georgia caught up with the group.

"What kind of name is Con, anyway?" asked Bobby. "I mean, what country does it come from?"

Con frowned just slightly in the shadows. "It's the capital of Turkey, turkey."

"I thought that was Istanbul," Bobby replied.

"Try calling yourself 'Isty,' O.K.?"

Chapter 16

Alva Van Buren kept her promises, no matter how easy it might have been to excuse herself under pressure. It was the one thing above all else her daughters admired, and which—when *they* were under pressure—comforted them: knowing that any and everything they confided would be kept confidential.

Their mother's steadfastness gave both Ava and Georgia a sense of security. Not that their lives were necessarily full of dark secrets or mystifying events. As Alva herself would remind them both from time to time, it was their very humanness that made them so valuable in the world, the things they had in common with other girls: problems, successes, failures. And of course these were what enabled her, Alva, to be of such service to them both.

Every Wednesday, Alva Van Buren walked down to the public library, through rain or sleet or knee-deep snow, to spend hours there reading the Sunday *New York Times,* section by hefty section. It was she who lined up her family in front of its television set for *Masterpiece Theatre,* insisting always that watching a dramatization of a book was only an introduction to, not a replacement for, the actual reading experience. She was a member of the Book-of-the-Month Club, an organizer for the annual Planned Parenthood book sale of Owanka's county, and lent her warm alto voice to the Owanka Renaissance Chorale.

It was she who decided when and where to take family vacations, helping to squeeze her three children and husband into her van to head downriver to see Mark Twain's home and museum in Hannibal, Missouri, or to drive hundreds of miles to the Southwest to explore the Native American cultures of the Hopis and Zunis in Arizona and New Mexico, or to amble slowly along the Cumberland Trail or among the Smokies, up to Gettysburg and then down again to Williamsburg on a Colonial America swing.

One afternoon Ava returned from school to find her mother sitting in the kitchen, reading and having a cup of tea. She shrugged off her coat and approached Alva, having no fear of criticism or belittlement as she handed her mother the latest copy of the Owanka *Hawk* in which her own front-page article ran. She also knew she was not likely to be praised beyond belief.

Her mother bent her head to read. "I like your title," she said immediately. "It's catchy but not too cute."

Ava nodded silently. "'Grapes Still Sour.'"

Her mother continued to read in silence. Soon she was finished. She looked up at her older daughter. "So?"

"So," Ava said just a little hesitantly, "it's not good enough."

Her mother smiled. "That's a very healthy attitude."

"I don't mean it's *not* good," Ava explained. "Just that it probably could have been a lot better, a lot stronger." She shrugged off her shoulder bag and dug for a second or two deep within it. She pulled out a folded piece of paper, which she handed to her mother.

Alva Van Buren ducked her head to this task, too. When she finished reading, she put the newspaper clipping aside. "You have different audiences, dear," she said.

"I know, I know," Ava agreed. "But next to that, my work seems so . . . so . . . well, timid."

"I don't think so," replied her mother. "You're reporting what went on. That's your job."

"But isn't it my job too to direct people?"

"What do you mean?"

"Well, I know the press is supposed to be independent and nonjudgmental, but the really good reporters have points of view, have feelings just like their readers. That's what makes them so good. They can tap into their own feelings, knowing that their readers will understand because they agree. And if they don't agree, isn't it the reporter's task to help them understand?"

"Understand what?" asked Ava's mother. "Understand how the reporter feels, or convince them that what the reporter feels is the only way a reasonable human being could feel?"

Ava couldn't help but laugh. "Well—"

Alva smiled. "You know, dear, it's the details that count, that help your readers understand where you stand. It's the things you choose to use that tell them about you." She paused to reach out for Ava's piece from *The Hawk*.

"This, for instance," she continued. "'I've never been involved personally in anything like this before,' said Ms. McCandless after the meeting. 'But the American Library Association has, and this approach to complaints and their value has been found useful. I doubt very much whether anyone would question the value of the book as much as its form. I'm sure teachers and librarians would be happy enough to substitute if they could find something equally distinguished.' Don't you think your point of view is pretty clear, Ava?"

Ava thought about this for a second. "Maybe. Then how come no one says anything to me about it?"

"You mean, no one complimented you?"

"I guess."

"Ava, you're doing your job. People expect you to write well. They don't expect you to set off bombs."

"But look what's in *The Herald*," Ava objected. "*She* gives historical background. She mentions other cases of censorship. She talks about the influence of pressure groups. I mean, it's so much fuller!"

Ava's mother nodded. "And she has pictures and

graphs. What she has, dear, that you don't—at least now—is resources. Remember, you're reporting for your peers."

"You don't think my peers can read graphs?"

"I don't mean that, dear. What I mean is that a professional is exactly that, a professional. She, or he, has been hired because he or she knows how to use resources to make his writing valuable to a community. But your community needs to be serviced, too, dear, and that's what you're providing. You're looking at what happens with the eyes of your friends. Maybe you expect too much from yourself."

Ava shook her head. "It's not that, Mom. I'm not beating myself over the head because I'm not a professional. I'm beating myself up because I don't know what I think yet, where I stand, and it shows!"

Chapter 17

Georgia blew into her front hall, leaving the door wide open behind her. Without shedding her jacket, she ran into the livingroom where she knew she would find Ava and Martin Brady. The scowl on Ava's forehead was a sign of triumph, as far as Georgia was concerned. She had her sister's attention.

"I've brought someone by who wants to meet you, desperately!" Georgia announced happily.

Ava's eyes went ceilingward. "Who might that be?" asked Martin, having moved a few inches away from Ava's side on the sofa.

"You'll never guess!" Georgia teased. She looked back over her shoulder. "Come and sign in, mystery guest, please!" she shouted.

Susan Woods crossed the Van Buren threshold, a lightweight cashmere sweater thrown over her shoulders, her thin lips parted in a broad, generous smile. She stepped forward into the room as Martin stood up.

"I'm so glad to meet you," Susan Woods said, offering her hand to Ava who sat still on the couch. "I'm Susan Woods. I work for *The Herald.*"

Ava stood finally and shook the reporter's hand. "This is my friend, Martin Brady," she said after a second. "Obviously, you know my sister, Georgia."

Susan Woods smiled again and nodded. "She's becoming quite famous, your sister," she offered. "A real fireball."

There was a moment of awkwardness before Ava suggested that her guest sit. As Ms. Woods passed Ava to take a chair at the end of the settee, Ava noticed she was just the slightest bit overweight. But she wore clothes with a real flair, and her complexion was so creamy it would be the envy of anyone.

"Can I get you anything, Sue?" Georgia asked, assuming the role of hostess. "Coffee, a soft drink?"

"Coffee would be nice, if it's no bother."

"Who's that?" shouted Jonny from the top of the stairs. "Who are you all talking to?"

"Never mind," Ava replied. "Go back to bed. Mom and Dad will be back in a few minutes."

Shuffling footsteps from upstairs could be heard below as Jonny returned to his bedroom.

"I promise I won't stay long," Susan Woods said next. "So let's just get right down to business, O.K.?"

Ava shot a puzzled look at Martin.

"You did a good job on the council meeting, Ava," Susan Woods judged. "I was very impressed."

Ava nodded, reddening just the slightest.

"I think we should work together," said Ms. Woods then.

Georgia reentered the livingroom and stood listening, a look of pride spread over her features.

"You do?" Ava finally said.

Susan Woods nodded. "What I mean is this: I can attend town meetings, or do interviews, but you're right there on the scene, on the battlefield. Without your dispatches from the front, I'm just covering half the story. That's simply not good enough."

"I really don't think I can help all that much," Ava said thoughtfully. "Most kids aren't that concerned, really."

"But it's more than just the students in your class or Georgia's," Susan Woods explained. "It's what's happening among the teachers, too. I mean, they're not only teachers. Many of them are parents, too. They'll have their personal views which, it seems to me, will be impossible to separate from their professional views."

"I don't think they'll share much of what they feel with *me*," Ava said honestly.

"They may not have to," Susan Woods said rather slyly. "You're perceptive. You're literate. You're more than smart enough to read the signs for yourself and to draw conclusions."

Ava frowned slightly. "Is drawing conclusions fair? In writing for a newspaper, I mean. After all, theoretically,

I'm just supposed to report the news, no frills. Wouldn't drawing conclusions, as you say, be sort of immoral?"

Susan shook her head. "Here's a little trade secret," she offered. "It's just as impossible for reporters to keep their personal biases out of their work as it is teachers, no matter how hard we try. Even the selection of the features we do more or less indicates our sympathies."

"You mean your mind is already made up?" Ava asked.

"Of course it is," Susan replied smoothly. "It has to be. After all, what's at stake here isn't just one book or one set of opinions. It's the freedom of choice. And freedom of the press, too. I'd be cutting off my own nose if I didn't understand that. I *have* to make other people see it, too."

"The power of the Fourth Estate," Martin interjected softly.

Susan Woods nodded her agreement. "If a paper has acted responsibly, written and lobbied quietly and honestly over the years, people have a tendency to trust it. We bring the world into someone's home and tell him how it's going to affect him. We have a touch more objectivity than our readers because we try hard to look at the Big Picture. But what we're trying to do, underneath everything else and every day, is inform and persuade."

"That's what I keep telling her," Georgia inserted. "Ava has an obligation."

Susan Woods almost but not quite ignored this. She smiled coolly. "Now, getting down to cases, surely you know where you stand in all this?"

Ava was immediately embarrassed. She didn't want to lie. She nodded, as noncommittally as she could. "Although," she said after a moment, "I'm not the fire-brand Georgia is."

"Which, for our purposes, is just as well. After all, we want you to be discreet, subtle."

"Is Ava going undercover?" Georgia asked, agog.

Ms. Woods laughed. "Not exactly. But I want the sources. I want you, Ava, to keep notes on people you've heard or spoken with, in addition to what they're saying and thinking. Teachers, kids, Laura McCandless, anyone who opens up and volunteers. If you can *get* people to do that, that's even better. It's not as though you'll be sneaking around spying. You're covering the story anyway for *The Hawk*. You would just be giving me more resources, more information, so that the stories *The Herald* prints are fuller and better rounded than they might be."

Martin coughed quietly. "Will Ava get her own byline?" he asked. "Will she receive credit at all?"

Susan Woods looked quickly at Martin and then away just as quickly. "Naturally," she said firmly. "It may take a little time, of course. But there's no reason she shouldn't be acknowledged."

Ava stood up. She felt flattered and a little light-headed. "If what you're doing is worthwhile and you believe in it, why then, who cares about credit?"

Susan Woods stood as well. "Right!" she agreed happily. "That's the way we *all* feel."

"I'll be happy to help," Ava decided.

"The Woodward and Bernstein of Owanka!" Susan Woods decided with a contented grin on her face as she shook Ava's hand.

"Ricki Lake and . . . and Alicia Silverstone!" Georgia echoed enthusiastically, mixing her media.

"I'll call you in a few days," Susan Woods said, beginning to turn away at last. "We can do lunch on Saturday, if you're free."

"I work at *Chez Elle* on Saturdays," Ava explained.

"Perfect! That's just across the street from *The Herald*. I'll look forward to it."

As Ava and Georgia escorted Susan Woods to the front door, Martin stood in place, frowning.

Chapter 18

Saturday morning did not start out happily for Ava Van Buren.

Her father had gone to his hardware store. Her mother was driving Jonny around on errands. Georgia was somewhere, no doubt doing something that Ava wouldn't be caught dead doing in a million years.

She stood at the kitchen sink sipping tea and leafing through *The Herald*. She turned its pages slowly, looking at headlines, grateful that good lead writers spared her the time to actually read what was in each article. She turned to the editorial page because she loved the political cartoons.

> Gentlemen:
> As you have reported, there is a drive in our community to censor the freedom to read of Owanka's younger citizens.

Without making personal accusations of motive on the part of those members of the city council who approve and support this measure, we want others to know a choice does still exist, and can, if we all work together.

To that aim, we are soliciting support—moral as well as financial—for FIRIF (Freedom Is Reading Is Freedom). Inquiries and/or donations may be sent to me at the address below, or to Mr. Donald Arrand, c/o Owanka National Growers Bank.

Georgia Van Buren
V.P., FIRIF

Ava couldn't decide which emotion was assaulting her: mortification, embarrassment, or simple rage. It was one thing to have an activist in the family. It was something else again for her to embarrass that family beyond belief.

She tried to calm herself as she read farther down the "Letters" section.

Gentlemen:
There is a divisive, corrosive, and inflammatory movement organizing in Owanka of which you are clearly aware. I refer to the position taken by Mr. Fairchild Brady of the city council, et al., that he (and they) know what books are best for our children to read.

I have seen entire communities disrupted and destroyed by attempts at censorship such as this, extending even to trying to legislate or force whole families to conform to so-called community standards.

I urge every man and woman who believes in freedom and fair play and the right of personal choice on which this country is founded to fight Mr. Brady's proposition, and to vote, on November 6, to defeat his attempt to fiat fundamental freedoms in our city.

Urgently,
Rev. Robert E. Fickett, Ret.
Owanka Methodist Church

Chapter 19

Susan Woods was wearing a smile of glee as Ava slipped into a booth for lunch that day. "It's happening, Ava!" she said enthusiastically. "I knew it would take a few days, but boy-oh-boy! Are we going to have a battle royal on our hands!"

"What makes you so happy?" Ava asked. "I can see it's a good story, but I'm not sure it's anything to be joyous about."

"No, of course not," Susan hedged just a little, picking up her menu to scan it theatrically. "I don't mean to sound as though I'm gloating. It's just that this is the kind of story that can really explode, really give you a chance to show your stuff."

"Did you see the two letters in the paper this morning?"

Susan Woods nodded eagerly. "You wouldn't believe the ones we didn't print! Oh Ava, this is going to be such a carnival!"

"What happens if Mr. Brady wins?"

"But don't you see?" Susan asked in return, leaning across the table. "It doesn't make any difference. One way or the other we have a battle here that can echo all across the state, all across the country! I mean, you don't imagine Owanka is the only town in America to feel this way, do you?"

Ava shrugged. "I hadn't thought about it."

"Well, do!" Susan suggested happily. "The entire election is being fought on these very same issues. 'America's fallen on its behind . . . we have to return to the old values . . . America has to be what it once was, leader of the free world, caller of the shots, the most righteous, the strongest, the wisest . . .' I mean, that's what some pols are giving us. Make no mistake. What's going on here, Mr. Brady's crusade to clean up the schools, that's only a symptom of other conflicts across the country."

"You mean we're part of the Big Picture?" Ava asked, a tiny smile on her lips.

"Absolutely. Wait and see."

"You think Mr. Brady will win?"

Susan nodded. "Not enough to make bets on it yet, but probably."

"I wonder if Georgia sees all this the way you do."

"Probably not in the same terms. But you can bet your bottom dollar the Reverend Fickett sure does."

Ava grimaced. "I'm not sure his letter is going to do what he wants. Bringing a church into this, even writing its name at the bottom of a letter, well, that seems a little risky to me."

"Wait, wait," Susan Woods cautioned. "This is just the beginning. Churches all over are getting into politics. If one church takes a stand, another will have to. Then businesses and unions and families and you name it. In four weeks the whole town will be two armed camps.

"This kind of brouhaha is like a disease, Ava. It starts out as a slight fever, then a few aches develop. Then maybe pneumonia. Then a wild rash or seizures or . . . or who knows?"

"I don't understand."

"What I mean is that while what's happening just now seems to be about a *book*, what it does to people causes the whole argument to expand, to slop over into other issues. All the dirty or envious or secretly mean feelings people harbor about each other begin to swim to the surface. Suddenly a hundred other issues are on the table, and not all of them pretty."

Ava was genuinely puzzled. "But reading seems so . . . so, well, so harmless. I mean, it's just between me and a book. That's what FIRIF is all about."

Susan Woods smiled knowingly. "That's where it started, I give you that. But that isn't where it will end."

"Did you know the Bradys are Methodists?"

"Ohmygod!" Susan laughed, clapping her hands. "What a face-off!"

Ava frowned. "You make this sound like *fun*."

"But it is!"

Chapter 20

"Has he kissed you?"

"Charlotte! Get a grip!"

"I'm calm. I'm always calm. Just answer the question."

Georgia wasn't sure what to reply. She held the telephone receiver a little way from her ear, thinking. For her part, on the other end of the line, Charlotte knew exactly what Georgia was doing.

"No," Georgia said at last. "Not yet."

"Well, what are you waiting for?"

"Charlotte, these things take time," Georgia said, thinking she sounded wimpish.

"The man's been around the world, Georgia. I mean, he certainly knows how to make a move."

"Con's not like that."

"Are you telling me you're his first?"

"First what?"

"First anything. He's sixteen, Georgia. Surely he's had plenty of opportunities."

"This doesn't sound like you, Charlotte. Really."

"I know. I don't understand it myself. Maybe it's just that I think falling in love is wonderful . . . supposed to be wonderful, anyway. I'm an only child, remember. Who am I going to talk to if not to you?"

"Well, I'm sorry, but I haven't got anything to report. It's too soon." Georgia grinned into her receiver. "Besides, what would happen to my reputation if people found out?"

"There's nothing to find out."

"Yet. That's all I'm saying. Yet. You may tell the press that we are just good friends."

"But that's true."

"So far, Charlotte. So far."

Chapter 21

The night was a warm one. Owanka was having a spell of Indian summer and the early October air was sweet with the scents of leaves and cut grass and late-blooming climbing roses.

Ava and Georgia Van Buren ambled along the sidewalk, leading down from Donald Arrand's hilltop home where another meeting for FIRIF had just been held. Ava had accompanied her sister as "press," an official observer. She had taken no part in the planning and discussion, in the critiques of progress so far and what was to be hoped between then and the election only a few weeks away.

Rather than continue to think about censorship and how to fight it, and Fairchild Brady, both girls seemed to want a rest. Ava was old enough to sense this and to take advantage of it. "So," she began slowly, "who is this Con Arrand?"

Georgia shrugged coolly. "Mr. Arrand's nephew."

Ava smiled to herself in the shadows. "Is that all? All to you, I mean?"

"Give me a break!" Georgia said, trying to sound disgusted but not succeeding. "He's only here until his family gets things organized where they are. In North Africa, if you want to know."

"Oh?" Ava waited. Like Charlotte Bracken, she knew that Georgia couldn't be stopped once her mind was on "charge."

"Yes, oh," Georgia mimicked. "If you have to know, he's here for only a little while. Then he's off to join his mother and father in the diplomatic service."

"He seems to like you," Ava took a faltering step into the unknown.

"Probably," Georgia replied. "He might."

"And you?"

"Me? For heaven's sakes, Ava, he's almost an office temp!"

"What do you mean?"

"What I mean is, he's certainly not someone I can focus on. He'll be gone as fast as I make up my mind. I mean, talk about a poor investment in time and effort!"

Ava walked a little in silence. "I think I remember him," she decided.

"You might. He's been here before."

"He's a couple of years younger than I am, isn't he?"

Georgia nodded.

"He's very attractive, Georgia," Ava said.

"I know."

"And he seems bright."

"I know."

"And he seems rather stuck on you."

"Ava, give it a rest, will you? I've just told you, he doesn't fit into my plans. He can't even vote!"

"Neither can you."

Silence split the two girls then. Georgia was pleased imagining she had deflected Ava's accurate estimate of what might or might not be developing between herself and Con Arrand.

Ava let the matter drop, imagining that what had just been exchanged with her sister would in time pay off, lead Georgia toward a little more softness and to taking what might, really, be her first real personal choice. Georgia was, had always been, terrific about getting involved in abstractions, in ideas and causes. But Ava had never felt her quite so anxious to enter the arena of real human feeling, the kind that could be exchanged between two separate beings. After all, she reminded herself, Georgia *was* young.

Ava chose instead to consider how in just a short time *The Grapes of Wrath* had overtaken her town. For one thing, without meaning to, Mr. Brady had opened cellar doors, and candidates for the city council—all running against him—had emerged into the light.

The election itself was simple. Anyone could announce his or her availability and make a run. Seats on the council were ultimately awarded to the five biggest vote getters.

One didn't need signatures of support or even a ten-dollar down payment on honesty. No one ran against anyone else, really. Each candidate said what he or she wanted and kept his or her fingers crossed.

The newcomers for this particular November were all write-ins, since ballots had been printed just a few days after Stanley Sopwith's research had been completed.

The races benefitted in intensity *because* of Mr. Brady's proposition, not in spite of it. The emotions unleashed by the two hearings in the town hall had drawn twenty candidates for five seats into the race.

As for those in Owanka who chose not to run, they found out suddenly that they cared very deeply—not only about reading and what was suitable for children to read, but also about the country's drift toward immorality, inequities in taxes, America's foreign aid ("handouts," some said), and the intrusion of government into everyone's daily lives (which, Ava thought, was mirrored exactly in Mr. Brady's proposal).

Ava had wanted to ask Mr. Brady just how he had come across *The Grapes of Wrath* in his younger son's bedroom to begin with. What was he really looking for? And how did poor Matt feel about the intrusion into his own private space?

On reflection, though, Ava had decided this was not the role of the press, unless one's newspaper was a supermarket tabloid.

On the Monday morning following the Saturday of Georgia's letter to *The Herald,* Mr. Arrand had come out of his house to get into his car to drive to the bank. What he found was that all four tires on it had been slashed during the night.

Mr. Arrand was a quiet, courteous, well-spoken man. He did not turn purple or shout. He went back into his house to call a taxi to get to the bank. For the next few weeks, his Mercedes stayed in his driveway, exactly as it had been that particular morning, and where it looked as though it were hunkering down on its haunches, deep in rather mournful thought. He left his car as a memorial, a reminder of what was happening to Owanka.

The current members of the council behaved just as everyone would have expected, depending on his or her personality.

Amos Allen made no speeches, went to no rallies, canvassed at no bazaars. His attitude was clearly stated in one of Susan Woods's articles in *The Herald*: "People know me. They know how I think. If they don't like it, they can make a change."

Mrs. Irene Clarke, always looking fresh and cool, flirting a little with her audiences, was dismayed that Owanka's once quiet, leafy streets should be littered by flyers and handouts, with harangues from loudspeaker trucks imported from Iowa City or Des Moines. She never for one minute wanted to say anything against Mr. John Steinbeck. She simply thought he had been ill-advised to let his imagination flow quite so freely.

The council's treasurer, Mr. Hubbell, refused to be drawn into any kind of discussion of the issue itself.

When interviewed, he simply said that he was a numbers-cruncher, and that whether he had done a good job was what the voters had to decide.

Mrs. George Nichols, who felt strongly that the issue was an affront to her school board's prerogatives and duties, spoke to the Rotary Club, the Kiwanis, the Chamber of Commerce. She would always begin by saying that the views of Fairchild Brady as well as his lieutenant, Stanley Sopwith—who was a suddenly energized write-in candidate—were barbaric, unreasonable, racist, chauvinist.

But it wasn't just Stanley Sopwith and Fairchild Brady Mrs. Nichols was after. She took on the Christian Coalition and the New Right, accusing them of backing the issue to benefit their own views of the world. She bemoaned the failure of Washington to provide leadership. Mrs. Nichols talked about Owanka but she was addressing the world. She was entering real politics, though most people didn't see this right away. For a time, some people just thought she had gone off the deep end.

Stanley Sopwith himself, clearly a founding father of the local New Right and, while not a member of the current council, therefore not seeking re-election, was invited to appear before the identical groups. He gave the same speech over and over, varying its emphases sometimes but always ending with a call to valor, patriotism, to America first, last, best and always.

Standing at the top of his particular Olympus gazing down at the mortals around him was Fairchild Brady, totally convinced that what he was doing was right. A lot of people agreed with him. What Mr. Brady was offering his followers was their first chance in years to change their own lives. While many voters may not have been overfond of Fairchild Brady, nonetheless they were serious about taking this first opportunity to Make a Difference, to Turn the Country Around, to start to slow Creeping Immorality and Public Dishonesty.

"You know, Ava, you can't very well keep—"

Georgia had broken into Ava's reveries and just as quickly Ava broke into Georgia's thought. "Listen, Georgia, it's not that I'm unimpressed by what *you're* doing, and how *you* feel. But you have to allow other people to make up their minds and vote however they will, and you must give me the same freedom."

The pair were only a few hundred yards from their home.

"Doesn't old Fairchild make you see red?"

"Getting angry is the last thing anyone needs," Ava defended. "The whole town's frothing at the mouth. The only person I've met recently who remembers he's a civilized human being is your friend Con."

Georgia was about to reply when Ava put her hand on Georgia's arm. The two stopped where they stood.

Lights were on in their home. That wasn't unusual. Nor was it strange that they should be able to hear the sound of voices within.

What was surprising was that they could hear the tone and rhythm of speech. They did not hear shouting. But

the tenor of their parents' voices rose and fell in a stac-
cato tempo, Fred Van Buren's slower and deeper in color,
Alva's rising and faster.

Both girls took a step nearer their front door.

"But she's right!" their mother said. "I mean, my God,
Fred, of course you can see that!"

". . . be right for herself . . . not making judgments like
that."

"That is just cowardice!"

"Alva, listen to yourself. You don't mean that."

". . . probably not . . . but what about what we believe
in . . . years and years?"

"Are you talking about choice?" Fred Van Buren asked.

Georgia, beside her sister, was rigid.

"Well, of course I am!" Alva Van Buren argued, her
voice rising again.

"Well then, remember please that choice extends in
both directions. I have as much right to my choice as
Georgia does to hers."

"Fred, can you honestly sit there and tell me with a
straight face that you believe censorship is a good thing?"

"I'm not discussing censorship."

"You certainly are! There just isn't any other word.
What you're advocating is censorship, pure and simple."

"What I'm advocating is the reasonable expectation of
any parent to protect his children from what he thinks is
harmful."

"Georgia is thirteen, for heaven's sakes. By the time
she gets to tenth grade, she'll be fifteen. You're not telling

me you think Ava was damaged irreparably by reading this book?"

Ava waited.

"No, I'm not," answered her father evenly. Then, after a second, he continued. "All I'm saying is that times have changed, and I'm not sure I like how they've changed. I want the children to see the old values cherished. I want them to grow up to become good citizens. I don't want them to see immorality and cheating and crime as everyday occurrences that have to be lived with."

"Come on!" Alva sounded exasperated. "You're just burying your head in the sand, Fred. You can't seriously believe that *The Grapes of Wrath* is going to color Georgia's perception of becoming an adult."

"Of course it will, just as any other book she reads will."

"Are you going to make her stop reading?" Alva asked.

"No. I'm just going to try to make certain that what she reads presents a picture of the world that I can live with."

"*You?*" Alva Van Buren nearly shouted. "*Your* picture of the world. Who are you trying to protect, yourself or Georgia?"

But Alva's husband ducked the question. "We're not such bad originals, Alva."

His wife laughed, but not unkindly. "Are you standing there telling me that your parents forced their view of the world onto their son? Think, Fred, *think!* You were the first Van Buren ever to go to college. Surely your parents had confidence in you, had some feeling that you were able to fend for yourself, make your own decisions, live with them?"

Georgia's father was silent.

"They trusted you to make your own friends, didn't they?" asked Alva then. "They let you choose me, for heaven's sakes. I mean, who knew then? Perhaps I would have corrupted you."

"And so you did," said Ava's father with a laugh just loud enough to be heard out of doors.

Georgia's entire frame was shaking. Ava held on to her arm tightly.

"Fred, this is my final word," said Mrs. Van Buren softly.

"Final as in Georgia's final?" teased her husband.

This was ignored.

"I can't stop you from voting for the proposal. I can't, and I wouldn't, stop you from talking with the children about this. But I think you ought to know that the way you feel is directly opposed to everything I've ever felt or thought or wanted from life. I don't believe in censorship. I don't believe books can be harmful to children. A child brings his own experiences to what he reads. If it's pornography he's got in front of him, unless he understands what's going on, sooner or later he's going to put the thing aside and get on with his life. I believe, Fred, and I mean this, I believe that words are precious and stories more valuable than gold. And if you carry this discussion outside this house, if you get up in church and take a public stand, then you are hereby on notice that I will do the same, more loudly, more angrily, and I'll campaign day and night. You'll learn to cook or starve. You'll learn to operate the washing machine, and to vacuum and to dust and to shop for food. And once I get going, who knows? Maybe I'll just sign on with Louise Nichols and work my way to the statehouse."

Mr. Van Buren laughed gently. "Now, that is censorship."

"You're damned right! This can cut both ways."

"Ohhh, Alva," said Georgia's father.

"Don't 'ohhh, Alva' me," Ava's mother replied.

"Ohhhh!" Georgia whispered, breaking Ava's grip and reaching out for the screen door. "I'm going to go in there and—"

Ava spun her around to a full stop. "If you even think of opening that door one little inch," she said, "I am going to make a real case for censorship and punch out your tiny brain!"

Chapter 22

Georgia did not sleep well. The words of her parents echoed in her memory.

She had never before heard them argue. When she thought about this, and she did, at two o'clock in the morning, she imagined that certainly they must have disagreed in all the years of their marriage. She, Georgia, simply had not been aware of any tensions between them. Probably, Georgia reasoned, if they did have an argument, they had it in private, out of the range of younger ears.

But to have heard them argue over what, to Georgia, was inarguable, was beyond her ability to understand.

At four that same morning, Georgia had made up her mind to work harder on her father, to show him more clearly where he was wrong, to help ease the tension between her father and her mother. For their own sakes.

At seven-thirty, when she was roused by her mother's insistent calls from downstairs, Georgia floated amid another memory: the conversation between herself and Ava about Con Arrand.

Georgia pulled a pillow over her head and moaned.

What she had done instinctively was cover her own feelings, her own sense of disappointment. Because the words she had used to tell Ava that Con was not a part of any picture of life in the future were almost syllable for syllable those that Con himself had used before yesterday's meeting of FIRIF.

They had met in the school hallways after lunch, not accidentally but rather by Georgia's design. She had come to know Con's class schedule as well as her own, and daily she plotted to make public contact with him.

There were two natural reasons for her behavior: first, it pleased her every time she saw him; she liked the way he looked, the way he walked, the sound of his voice. Also, to be seen talking publicly with such a desirable boy did nothing to hurt Georgia's public image, which had, to be truthful, begun to suffer just a bit as she poured her energies into the fall election and FIRIF.

Her own friends, apart from Charlotte Bracken, seemed just ever so slightly to be easing off, easing away. Georgia's activism and certainty were more than her eighth-grade peers wanted to deal with. To most of them, what mattered more were Owanka's football team, movies at the mall, hanging out and flirting.

Georgia was determined not to run more slowly for

anyone. She had a finish line in view and anything and anyone that stood between her and it was likely to be bowled over and left forgotten in the dust.

On the other hand, to be seen with Con Arrand every day *somewhere* reminded her friends that Georgia was still a young woman who was found attractive by a young man, who was also found attractive by more girls than only Georgia. A few of these casually inquired about him as days passed, and Georgia was only too glad to be able to stand in the center of a circle of her peers, playing coy but also teasing at the same time.

How much of all this Con himself understood Georgia did not know, and had not yet considered. She knew he liked her. She knew he felt comfortable with her. She knew other girls were jealous. Con, after all, was two grades ahead.

After greeting each other in the hallway, Con's face became somber as he looked down at Georgia. "What?" she asked, worried. "What?"

"I got a letter from my dad yesterday," Con replied.

"So? How is he? How's your mom?"

Con nodded. "They're both fine. He wrote to tell me that . . . that he thought I might be able to fly over to join them around Thanksgiving."

At first Georgia had not reacted. She kept looking up into Con's eyes, cool and soft behind his glasses, waiting. When he didn't add anything immediately, she blinked.

"Oh," was all she could think to say at first.

Con nodded again.

Georgia took a big breath and with effort smiled. "So, then, what does this mean? Really?"

Con had shrugged. "I don't know," he began. "I just thought I should tell you."

A bell rang somewhere in the building. They were going to be late for their next classes. The spaces around them emptied.

Con suddenly grinned, a little. "I guess you could call me an office temporary," he said.

"What?"

"Well, in your life, I mean," he explained.

Georgia was still in shock.

"After all," Con said, easing into the silence, "it's not as if we hadn't known this would happen."

Georgia nodded, numb.

"Well," Con Arrand decided, hitching up his books and notebooks.

Georgia was still speechless. Con Arrand had no idea how rare this was. He turned to start to walk to his class.

"Wait!" Georgia called softly.

Con stopped and turned back.

"What exactly are you saying?" Georgia demanded.

Con shrugged. "I'm not the best investment you could make, Georgia. In time and effort. I mean, there doesn't look like there's any payoff in the future."

Georgia seemed to have awakened at this. "What payoff?" she asked, getting just the tiniest bit angry. "What payoff? And why do we need one in view, anyway? Can't we just go on, can't we still like each other? I mean, this isn't the only time in our lives we'll meet, is it? Probably."

"Probably, you're right," Con agreed.

"Well, then," Georgia had said, taking the few paces that separated them, "I don't see what this is all about. I'm glad your parents are safe. I'm glad they want you with them. I'd want my kids with me, too. I don't see anything at all unusual in this, in any of it."

And before Georgia could think what she was doing—before Con could take evasive action—Georgia went up on tiptoe and kissed Con on the cheek.

Con was later for his class than Georgia was for hers.

Chapter 23

Georgia stepped out of the shower, wrapping a warm towel around herself. She leaned across the sink and swiped at the mirror, clearing some of its mist. Then she stood back and regarded herself.

She smiled at her image. She really did think she was growing up a bit. Not just physically, although there was hope for that, as well. More importantly, she felt herself beginning to *think*.

First of all, there was only one thing to do about what she had heard the night before, the argument between her parents. She had changed her mind. It wasn't her business. There was nothing she could say that wouldn't make matters worse. She would just have to bite her tongue and plot to make points with her father. She was convinced that she alone could persuade him his point of view was . . . well . . . underdeveloped.

As for her mother, Georgia instinctively felt that she was perfectly capable of handling anything her husband handed her. She had always been, as far as Georgia could recall. She didn't need help or comfort or understanding.

Georgia closed her mouth and smiled thin-lipped into the mirror.

Not a bad look.

As for Con Arrand, what she had said in response to his dire warning of lovers forever separated pleased her as she remembered it. She felt very adult, and she giggled when she thought of her own bold kiss. *That* should hold him!

She raised a hair-dryer and switched it on, sweeping the machine around her damp curling red hair. She reasoned with herself. If the relationship between her parents was as good and solid as it had always been—after all, people are free to disagree from time to time—and if Con had been as startled by her kiss as she chose to think, then she could return to what really mattered: FIRIF. There was time to let him think.

Later she would entwine all three strands of her life into a vine that was strong and would hold against almost anything she could imagine. And, in the long view, as Charlotte would have said, what mattered most?

There wasn't any doubt of the answer to that question!

Georgia bounded down the stairway and rushed, as was her custom, into the family kitchen. She had had a further brainstorm for Ava, which she knew immediately had to be presented to her sister very slyly.

The press, the *national* press, had been inching into

Owanka slowly, their numbers growing as the word crossed the country that Owanka was a perfect example of national trends toward local control of school boards and whatever funds they were allotted. It wasn't just another story of devout right-wing people plotting a takeover of the board. This was somehow larger: religion was only a part of what was happening.

The election in Owanka was beginning to be built up in the media as a perfect example of states' rights. What the national government wasn't directed to have (in the Constitution), it shouldn't have. Local control was what mattered.

Censorship mattered as well, since the press would always be among the first to feel the censor's restriction. There were other cities and towns that had struggled over individual book titles, or movies, or even television shows, but Owanka—being in the center of the country—was thought somehow to have something extra special to tell the country at large. It was too good an example of what Americans were thinking, how they were thinking, what divided them.

Georgia herself had been nabbed in school hallways, along the sidewalk in front of her own home, emerging from a meeting of FIRIF for quotes and interviews. No doubt her own growing presence was an irritant to Ava who was, after all, older, prettier, probably smarter, and who thought of herself as a member of the press—one of the people who selected what was to be written about as well as wrote it.

Others had become temporary focuses of the press as well. Mr. Brady presented himself as a saintly village elder, soothing and advising and protecting. Mr. Nagle upheld the opposing view rather less elegantly but more forcefully. Ms. McCandless tried always to keep the whole matter in perspective, and to give the battle in Owanka a sense of history.

But what Georgia had hit upon as she dressed upstairs, and even as she did she knew how carefully it had to be handled, was an "angle" of the whole Owanka story that hadn't yet been covered. And of course, in Georgia's mind, it should go to Ava.

That, of course, was the touchy thing. How to drop the idea on her sister in a way that would allow Ava to pick it up, turn it in the light, and pronounce herself pleased. Better, announce that she herself had had the most wonderful idea.

Ava was standing by the sink, her back against its board, finishing her orange juice. Georgia crashed into the room and slowed immediately, cautioning herself. She pretended to busy herself pulling open an English muffin and putting it in the toaster-oven.

After a suitable pause, Georgia turned around to face her sister. "Know what, Ave?"

Ava didn't speak. She simply looked at her sister coolly.

Georgia was not to be deterred. "You've probably thought about this yourself, I bet." She smiled.

"What?"

"Mr. Claffin."

Ava continued to stand motionless. "What about him?" she asked finally.

"Well," Georgia began, choosing her words carefully, "you probably thought about this whole thing and decided to wait until the time is right, didn't you?"

"I might have," Ava allowed, her curiosity just the slightest bit audible in her voice.

"I mean, what does he think? Is he going to cave in? You know, questions like that. I mean, who could be more central to all this than the teacher who assigned *The Grapes of Wrath* in the first place?"

Ava nodded her agreement, subtly. It wouldn't do to let Georgia think, even for one minute, that the suggestion was one she *hadn't* thought of. But should have, she scolded herself inwardly. She should have!

Chapter 24

Mr. Claffin was a man of nearly thirty, newly married and with a small baby boy. He had come to Owanka from the school system in Clinton, not too far to the east. To Ava, he seemed shy and boyish, almost surprised that someone should come to ask him what he thought about anything.

"Well," Ava said, sitting down across from him in his classroom, at last full of the fire she thought a reporter should demonstrate, "you surely lit a gigantic fuse."

He blushed and shook his head. "Not really. The book was on the syllabus already. It seemed to me a good read. I simply assigned it."

"When was the last time you read the book, all the way through?" Ava asked.

"I read everything before we study it," Mr. Claffin replied. "If I started to rely on notes or lectures or ideas

I'd used before, I'd bore myself and I'd bore my classes. Besides, when you reread something like this, new ideas always surface."

"Were you ever disturbed by the language in the book?"

Mr. Claffin shook his head. "Steinbeck doesn't start out swearing on page one. He leads you into the lives of his characters and then lets you listen to them speak. There are whole chunks of the book—mostly about Ma Joad—where there's no profanity at all."

"Would you assign the book again if you could?"

Mr. Claffin smiled. "Ah, well, you mean, if I knew what was going to happen, would I?"

Ava nodded.

"I'd like to think I would, Ava," said the teacher. "Honestly, though, I'm not sure. A lot of strange things have happened since all this began."

"What do you mean, strange?"

"The usual sorts of intimidation, you know."

"No, I don't know," Ava admitted flatly. "What?"

Mr. Claffin's grin was just a little sheepish. "Late-night telephone calls, anonymous letters, that sort of thing."

"Really? But why? Who?"

"Who I can't tell you. The why is anybody's guess. After all, what damage is real has already been done. I'm out of it now, effectively. I mean, it's unlikely that I'll assign anything I think might be controversial in the future. At least for a while, anyway."

Ava wanted to shout! That's the story!

"I guess," Mr. Claffin continued rather sadly, "people just like to feel powerful and threatening and strong, and if it gives them pleasure, why, I guess I can stand it."

"But what about your wife, your baby?"

"My wife's a little nervous, but that will pass, I'm sure."

"But this is awful!" Ava declared. "I mean, I can see someone threatening Mr. Brady or someone else, but not a teacher!"

Mr. Claffin smiled genuinely, as though he were remembering his youth. He said nothing more.

Chapter 25

Georgia began bringing her battle home with her every afternoon in the guise of one new friend after the other. Some were students. Some were grown-ups. The school's Reading Club meetings were shifted from its library to Georgia's den, and Alva dutifully prepared hot chocolate and soda and cookies for the group whenever Georgia ushered them through her front door.

Jonny's attitude toward these late-afternoon invasions never varied: he grabbed something from the refrigerator and spun on his heels to spend time outside until dinner and a return to normalcy.

Ava's and Georgia's classmates continued going to school, continued to struggle over world history quizzes and French and math. Martin and his weight-lifting cronies practiced football every afternoon on the field behind school, and they played games on Friday nights or

Saturday mornings, depending on the schedule and the weather. Owanka was having a good season. By the middle of October, it had won four games and lost only one.

Kids continued to hang out at different houses or the mall. They saw movies and listened to CDs. They completed homework assignments on time, or didn't. Some helped Georgia and Mr. Arrand and Mrs. Nichols when they had the time, or more realistically, when someone else they liked was going to do the same.

The air that autumn was filled not with burning leaves but politics. People who ordinarily had not a care in the world became suspicious and worried and began to find ogres under beds that had long since been forgotten. Mrs. Beaman, Ava's boss at *Chez Elle,* could hardly wait for customers to leave so she could instruct Ava in what every young woman should know.

"Now, I don't mean you should be paranoid, Ava," Mrs. Beaman announced one Saturday. "But it's only common sense for an attractive girl like yourself to be armed in *some* way."

Ava nodded silently.

"Really, women like us have to be constantly alert," Mrs. Beaman continued then, reaching behind a counter to lift her purse. She dipped into it and pulled out a can of Mace. "You never know when you might need this," she said, waving it in the air in front her breasts.

Ava tried not to smile. In her mind, the man who "desired" Mrs. Beaman was already blind.

But Mrs. Beaman was no more upset than others.

Suddenly she was wild to organize a center to counsel rape victims and to raise money for the Patrolmen's Benevolent Society.

"We simply have to tell the criminals that we won't take it any more," she would say. "What this country needs is to get tough, to force people to fear us again. Just because we try to be nice to all of them doesn't mean we can be kicked in the teeth!"

Mrs. Beaman—comfortable, round, not uneducated—was only a part of a population made nervous by what she saw on television, by what she read in her news weekly and watched on CNN. Fairchild Brady's campaign confirmed her direst fears. While she had never been a victim of any kind, had never had an incident she could recall with one of "them" (whichever "them" was under discussion), she knew her time was limited. Sooner or later it would happen and then people would see, oh yes!

That particular Saturday, when Ava returned from her half day's work at the shop, Alva was holding out the telephone toward her. Ava smiled and took the receiver.

"How could you do that to me!"

It was Susan Woods.

"I mean, Ava, it was dynamite. But why would you keep it from me?"

Ava grinned, just a little. "Well, how did I know what he would say?"

"You had plenty of time afterward," Susan Wood said rather curtly. "You could have reached me."

John Neufeld

"I only promised to *help*," Ava said firmly, thinking with gratitude of Mr. Claffin. "I didn't promise to turn over everything. Am I going to be subpoenaed? You want my notes?"

"Very funny," Susan retorted. "You know, Ava, I'm not sure what this does to our working relationship."

"Why should it do anything?" Ava asked innocently. "After all, you could have interviewed the man, too, if you'd thought of it."

There was a momentary silence on the line. "Well, promise me you won't go off on your own this way again," Susan suggested, rather weakly, Ava thought.

"I can't promise that," Ava said honestly. "But next time I'll give you fair warning, O.K.?"

Another pause. "I guess it will have to be."

Susan did not say good-bye.

Chapter 26

Georgia Van Buren was a wheeling, dealing, maddened field marshal during the final three weeks of the election campaign. She and Mr. Arrand and Mrs. Nichols had divided the city into eight sectors. Each afternoon teams from FIRIF were dispatched onto the streets and walkways of the small Iowa community. If time wasn't found during the day for Georgia's younger troops to get their daily assignments during school, a mob of *almost* equally dedicated soldiers arrived at her home.

Not only did young people show up, but adults as well. Men and women would take time off from work to campaign, collecting handouts and bumper stickers and pamphlets at three-thirty and then heading out onto the battlefield to do hand-to-hand combat with the forces of Repression and Evil. Many of these troops were older, retired people whose children had long since left Owanka for more enticing climes. And some were simply surprises to the organizers of FIRIF: people no one seemed to know or ever to have noticed, but who used the public library as both source and haven.

Ava decided one afternoon that to broaden her own experience of the war being fought, she herself should accompany one of Georgia's teams out onto the street. When she returned from school she found a dozen people milling in her mother's kitchen, waiting for their assignments, forming teams, making plans.

To Ava's astonishment, none of Georgia's troops—most of whom were older, wiser, more experienced than their general—ever challenged her or argued. Georgia's word was gospel. Of course, it was backed up by Mr. Arrand's and Mrs. Nichols's. Still, Ava was proud of her sister, realizing this sentiment even as she decided she must never in any way—as a *journalist*—let this creep into her stories.

Alva Van Buren provided hot chocolate and coffee and cookies. There was never an afternoon when she tired or grew short-tempered. She greeted her friends warmly and their children with respect, made simple suggestions that Georgia duly considered, and always lent encouragement to Georgia's army.

"O.K.!" Georgia called, striding into the kitchen, dropping her schoolbooks on the table there and scooping up a handful of Hershey's Kisses from a bowl Alva had put out. "Enough chit-chat. We've got work to do." The room quieted.

"Today we hit Sector Four," Georgia announced, drawing from her shoulder bag a sheaf of papers. "Charlotte, you and your mother go out with Mr. Wilson. Mrs. Fickett's with Mrs. McCord. Ava—Ava? Are you gracing us with your presence for a reason?"

Ava blushed. "For my readers," she said. "Once."

Georgia nodded, all business. "Right, then. You can go with Mrs. Putnam and Eddy."

"Eddy" was Edward Lyon Tabott, the oldest in a family of six boys, all of whom had long been considered retarded, or at least confused. Ava nodded at him and at Mrs. Putnam, a pleasant woman of thirty with two preschoolers waiting out in her car.

The troops were dismissed and Ava followed them all out onto the street, getting into the front seat of Mrs. Putnam's station wagon as Eddy climbed in back with her children.

The front seat was clear but the floor at Ava's feet held an enormous box filled with bumper stickers, pamphlets, campaign buttons, questionnaires and pledge forms. Also, of course, sharpened pencils and a box full of change.

Within a few minutes, Mrs. Putnam guided her car toward a curb and organized. Ava followed her and Eddy up a front walk to wait, standing to one side in order to listen to what was said and yet not intrude in any way. Mrs. Putnam rang the front doorbell and after a few moments a pleasant-enough looking woman Ava didn't recognize came to the front door. She opened it and stood inside the screen door, smiling.

"Mrs. Fawcett?" asked Mrs. Putnam. The woman nodded. "We're out campaigning to keep a book called *The Grapes of Wrath* on our high school's reading list. You've probably read something about all this in *The Herald?*"

Mrs. Fawcett nodded, still smiling.

Mrs. Putnam nodded in return. "We were hoping you would help our cause, which is really the cause of freedom to read what people want, after all. We'd certainly appreciate your help, in one way or another. I'd like to ask you to campaign in the neighborhood for us."

Mrs. Fawcett's smile wavered. "I'm not much good at soliciting," she admitted.

"No, just among your own friends, actually," Eddy Tabott said then. "Sort of rev them up, inform them what's at stake."

"I imagine they know about as much as I do already," said Mrs. Fawcett.

"Well then, perhaps you'd care to help in another way?" Mrs. Putnam suggested. "We need funds to advertise and to get our message across to the voters of Owanka. For only a dollar you could have a bumper sticker, or for fifty cents a campaign button."

She held out both items so that Mrs. Fawcett could see them. Mrs. Fawcett saw them. There was a moment of silence. "Well, I suppose," Mrs. Fawcett said at last, "I suppose I could take a sticker."

"That's wonderful," Mrs. Putnam said, trying to sound enthusiastic.

"If you wouldn't mind," Eddy added, "you could also answer some questions for us, if you would."

"Oh no, I couldn't do that," Mrs. Fawcett said hurriedly. "Be right back."

She turned and ducked away from the doorway. When she stood erect again in full sight, she held a dollar bill. But she didn't open her door.

There was an awkward moment before she realized that the money offered wasn't magical enough to pass through solids. She laughed self-consciously and blushed and opened the screen door just enough to slip out the bill, which Eddy took. In exchange, he squeezed her bumper sticker through the slit.

"We're having a rally, you know," Mrs. Putnam said quickly, before Mrs. Fawcett could turn away again. "The night before the election. We'd be thrilled if you'd come to it, and maybe bring your husband."

"Oh no, I couldn't do that."

"Well, if you change your mind," Mrs. Putnam told her, "at least you'll see a few friendly faces."

Mrs. Fawcett smiled sort of idiotically at this, Ava thought. There seemed nothing more to be said. Mrs. Putnam nodded her good-bye and together the three campaigners turned to walk back to the car.

"She'll never use the sticker," Eddy guessed.

Ava was amused, and a little shamed, to have thought Eddy Tabott so dense.

"I know," Mrs. Putnam agreed rather sorrowfully. "Still, we did get a dollar."

"That's not much," commented Ava.

"No, but if we got that from every house, we'd be rolling," Mrs. Putnam stiff-upper-lipped. Smiling, she started her car and glided down the street to stop before another house.

Once again the three emerged from the car. Ava examined the house they approached. In its driveway was a battered green sedan on whose back bumper were the fluorescent words LOVE IT OR LOSE IT!

Ava couldn't decide whether they were about to walk into a lion's den or the welcoming arms of a cohort. She chose discretion and said nothing, waiting to see.

Mrs. Putnam rang the doorbell, but it was Eddy Tabott who stood front and center as a middle-aged woman, wearing jeans and a halter top and sneakers, came to the door. "Yes?" she asked rather dourly.

Eddy reddened. "Mrs. Raymond, we're neighbors from just across town, and we're very interested in—"

But Mrs. Raymond was clearly used to door-to-door canvassers. "I don't need any," she declared. "Sorry you wasted your time."

"But—" Eddy started to say.

Mrs. Putnam came to his rescue. "Mrs. Raymond," she said in almost as strong a voice as her antagonist, "we're not selling anything. We need your support."

Mrs. Raymond had turned away but hearing that someone *needed* her caused her to turn again and to stand inside her screen, waiting.

"You probably know," Mrs. Putnam rushed on, "about the special election on November sixth."

Mrs. Raymond nodded, unsmiling.

"Well, a great many people in Owanka feel that if a particular proposal should pass, we would be censoring the reading, the lives of our children."

"Not mine," Mrs. Raymond snapped.

"Pardon me?" said Mrs. Putnam, although Ava was certain she had heard clearly.

"Mine are grown, gone, flown the coop," Mrs. Raymond said.

"Oh, I see," Mrs. Putnam allowed. "Then for you it would be a matter of principle more than anything else."

Mrs. Raymond nodded. "It is," she said. "I think that book's trash!"

"You do? Have you read it?"

"Don't need to," Mrs. Raymond replied. "From what I hear, there's dirty words on every page. Now, I don't care what kind of book it is, what kind of story, but people just don't need to write dirty words."

"But don't you think, being a reasonable woman," Mrs. Putnam said soothingly, "that really to be fair you ought to look into it yourself?"

"Nope," Mrs. Raymond said quickly. "Me and Nick both agree. What's filth is filth. And as far as we can see, if you let people get away with putting that stuff out, you're just inviting ruin. This country's already on her knees. Our job's to get her back up again, standing tall. People I trust a whole lot more than I do you seem to think it's bad stuff, and that's good enough for me."

Mrs. Raymond paused then and looked sharply through the webbing of her screen, her eyes narrowing. "Where do you all live, anyway?" she asked. "You don't look familiar to me."

"Just across town," Eddy Tabott managed.

Mrs. Raymond squinted around at Ava. "You sure you're not some outside . . . agitator?"

Mrs. Putnam smiled. "Believe us. We all live here in Owanka. Eddy and Ava go to Owanka High."

"What's your church?" demanded Mrs. Raymond.

Mrs. Putnam laughed gently and answered the question. Then she added: "I guess there's not much point in asking you to support our cause, is there?"

"Nope," Mrs. Raymond agreed. "I don't guess there is. Better luck somewhere else."

She turned quickly away back into her own house, not closing the heavier oak door inside because of the afternoon's Indian summer heat.

"Well," said Mrs. Putnam, settling back into her car, "I believe that's called losing some."

Ava smiled but Eddy did not. "It's meanness, is what it is," he said under his breath. "Just meanness. Some people don't *want* to understand."

"The problem is, Eddy," said Mrs. Putman, starting

her car, "that people understand as much as they want to and then they stop listening. After all, it's far easier to make up your mind quickly, even if later you're proven wrong, than it is to listen to everything and everyone and then try to make an informed decision."

Chapter 27

"Martin, would you please just kiss me?" Ava asked.

Martin did, leaning over toward her in the front seat of his truck.

"Thank goodness," Ava sighed.

"What?"

Ava felt a trifle sheepish. "I guess that we both still want to," she said quietly.

"I'll always want to, Ave."

"Easy to say."

"Easy to prove."

They kissed again. They were parked, along with others of their age and class, under the trees that surrounded what was called the Old Pond. It was Friday night, following a pep rally for the football game to be played the next day.

Ava pulled back slowly, grinning.

"Now, what's that supposed to mean?" Martin asked.

"It just goes to show," Ava answered, "that the election is *not* the most important thing in the world."

"You know," Martin whispered in Ava's ear, "I'm proud of what you've been writing."

"You are?"

Martin kissed Ava once more, just lightly. Then he pulled back toward the steering wheel. "I'm proud of anything you write."

Ava smiled in the shadows. "That seems a little too broad just now."

"Why?"

"Well, I've been doing a lot of thinking. I think I should do one real killer. Tell people they can't ignore democracy, the Bill of Rights. You know."

"The problem is, Ave, that kids like us don't vote."

"You'll vote, Martin. You're eighteen."

"Well, it's kind of tough, with my old man and all. I'm not sure I even want to approach a voting booth. No matter what I do inside it, I'll be grilled outside, later."

Ava sighed. "I wish what I thought counted."

"It does, Ave! No matter what side you come down on, it counts. You're standing in the middle of this with a microphone at your fingertips. You might influence someone else like me who does get to vote for the first time."

Ava sighed, her attitude slewing one hundred and eighty degrees as in a gale. "I am so sick of all this."

"Look, Ave, it will be over soon. If Georgia and Mr.

Arrand win, no one gets hurt. If my father wins, half of the town steams."

Ava shook her head vigorously. "Owanka is just falling apart," she sighed. "I mean, I never thought of people here as good or bad, as friendly or mean. Now all we have is tension, tension, tension. I can't stand it!"

"Then help us get over it. Reason on the page. Convince us all."

Ava sat without moving.

"Are you thinking about it?" Martin asked.

"No," Ava answered almost bitterly. "Not anymore. Because it means I would be betraying the newspaper code of ethics. You just don't pick sides, Martin. You report as objectively as you can. That's my job. That's my duty."

"But you also have a personal du—"

"Martin, take me home now, will you? Please?"

Martin sighed and started the truck. In silence he and Ava drove before he decided he could speak again. "Ava?"

Ava was looking out her window. She did not answer.

They had driven two miles back toward Owanka when both heard what sounded like an explosion.

Martin pulled his truck to the side of the road and opened his window. Within a few more seconds, he and Ava could both see off to the south a red glow in the sky. What they saw was not a leaping flame but rather what seemed to be a large, *very* large, coal, glowing on the horizon. Martin turned his truck in that direction and began tracing a route toward the flickering behind trees that lined the road.

Martin turned finally down Drew Lane. A crowd of people stood in front of a pretty, well-kept white frame house. In its driveway was a burning hulk of a car, still smoldering, smoke billowing up and around and then out sideways toward the bystanders. Martin drove closer.

"For God's sweet sake!" he whispered at Ava. He stopped his truck and got out quickly.

Ava sat where she was, squinting through the windshield. She did not know whose house this was, or whose car, but suddenly, amid the crush of people standing around, she caught sight of black faces. She closed her eyes quickly, seeing behind her lids Charlotte Bracken.

She felt weak suddenly, and began to perspire. She watched as Martin approached the people near the drive, spoke to some of them, and then turned to walk back again toward her. He opened the truck's door and got back in, switching on the ignition and beginning to back away slowly. "No one was hurt," he said quietly. "They've called the fire department."

"Fat lot of good that will do!"

Martin glanced quickly at her but said nothing.

"*That's* what happens when an ordinary person takes a stand! Like it?"

"That's not true, Ava."

"Tell that to Charlotte Bracken's mother."

"It could have happened to anyone."

"You don't believe that, and neither do I!" Ava replied angrily, clutching the dashboard. "They were an easy target. The simplest. The meanest!"

"Ava, we don't know that."

"Oh yes we do! I know it! God knows who will get it next! The Blooms, maybe, or Sarah Weinstein."

"Come on!"

"I'm serious! It's just what Susan Woods told me. This isn't about censorship now. It's about every ugly feeling anyone has ever had. Finally, people have a chance to strike out at others they envy or hate or fear. And it's all O.K. now because the very air around us is full of permission. Suddenly it's O.K. to do more than burn up inside. It's O.K. to actually hurt someone for a 'good' cause. I mean, what's the difference between this and what happened in Oklahoma City?"

"Ava, this isn't like that, at all."

"It's not?!" Ava was nearly screaming. "You know what? It doesn't make any difference who did this! I hope I never find out! What I do know now is that people here are just like people everywhere else! Owanka isn't pretty and green and *isolated!* It's just as big and mean as New York or Chicago or . . . or—"

"Ava, come on. Don't jump to conclusions. After all, the police will be called into this."

"The police!" Ava shouted. "You don't think police vote?"

Then, before she knew what was happening, she had vomited all over the front seat of Martin's truck.

Chapter 28

"Morning, darling," said Ava's mother as she saw her daughter come blearily into the kitchen. "Are you starving or just nibbly?"

"Don't ask me to make decisions," Ava said, sliding onto a chair at the table.

Alva shrugged and smiled. "Well, the makings are available for whatever you want. The paper's right there, too."

Ava looked across the table and saw the front page of the weekend edition of *The Herald*. She was not surprised to see there a photograph of the Brackens' burned-out car, looking rather surprised and alone in their driveway.

Ava began to shake. She reached over to upend the entire paper onto the floor. The Brackens' car was all she had thought about since dawn. All the images she had

John Neufeld

seen on television for as long as she could remember had finally come to Owanka, had come to rest not more than half a dozen blocks away from her own home. Deep down, perhaps, Ava had expected something to happen, not necessarily now, but sometime. It was a rotten way to feel.

"Well now," said her mother, ignoring the pile of newsprint, "what's on your schedule for the day?"

Ava shrugged. "I think I'm going to call Mrs. Beaman and tell her I can't work at *Chez Elle* anymore."

"You are? Why?"

Ava shrugged, puzzled at her own decision. "It just seems that right now there are other things I ought to be doing."

"You'll miss the money."

"Maybe I'll just take a leave of absence until the election's over."

Mrs. Van Buren nodded as she began loading the dishwasher. "Well, perhaps you'd like to help Georgia and me today, then," she suggested without turning around.

"Doing what?"

"Collecting for today's auction."

"What auction?" Even to herself Ava sounded increasingly out of it.

"For the Brackens," Ava's mother explained over her shoulder. "Georgia is organizing a benefit to raise money for a new car."

Ava shuddered. "God, doesn't she ever stop?"

Mrs. Van Buren looked quickly at her daughter and

126

then bent back over the sink. "I think Georgia's idea is grand," she said positively. "I'm pleased she came up with it, and we're all doing what we can to help. After all, this is so sudden. I mean, what we need to do is almost super-human. We could certainly use your help."

"Even Daddy's?"

"Of course. Why not?"

Ava stared at her placemat. "Where is this auction going to be?"

"At the stadium," Ava's mother said. "Right after the game this afternoon."

"Really?"

"Ms. McCandless is arranging for it. The phone's been ringing off the hook. We're all scouring attics and basements, asking neighbors, looking high and low for decent things people might want to buy."

Ava's eyelids flickered. She was beginning to feel light-headed. She reached quickly across the table to take a piece of toast. She bit into it, asking around its crust, "Who did it?"

"No one knows."

"No wonderful terrorist organization has taken responsibility?"

"Darling, that isn't funny. This is Owanka, not the Mideast."

"You could fool me," Ava said morosely.

Mrs. Van Buren poured a cup of coffee for herself and sat down across from Ava. "You're really very upset by all this, aren't you?"

Ava nodded. "Aren't you? Who knows which neighbor went off the deep end? Who knows which person could go overboard next? I mean, how are we supposed to live with this?"

"The best we can," Alva Van Buren replied. "I'm as upset as you are. Everyone I know is. But there is *so* little any of us can do.

"I agree it's hell living here, not being able to assure ourselves we're as safe as we used to be. And I hate to say it, Ava, but there isn't any place that's as safe as it was. But that doesn't mean we can't try to help, does it? It doesn't mean we have to stay silent ourselves in the face of these deeds."

"Are you frightened?"

"No, I'm mad," said her mother. "As angry as I've ever been. I'm ticking away inside. Your father knows that. He's half terrified I'll explode somewhere publicly. And I might."

"But you seem so . . . so capable, so strong," Ava said.

"Not everyone can give way to hysteria. Besides, I really believe our side will win. Not just against violence, which is the thing suddenly staring us in the face. But censorship, too. I have to believe that. And" —Mrs. Van Buren reached across the table and took her daughter's hand— "so do you."

Ava looked stunned. "Even with everything going on in the country, even with the election?"

"Even now," answered her mother. "America has

never been short of sensible, decent people. I'm relying on them, I suppose, or on Owanka's fair share."

Ava shook her head. "I don't know. You're sure, and Georgia's sure, and Daddy's just as convinced on his side. Someone's wrong here somewhere."

Chapter 29

The stands at the field behind Owanka High were half full. The day was overcast and chilly. If one had a choice, one stayed at home and listened to the game on the radio.

The afternoon wore on into shadowy half-light, and Owanka won the game. But the odd thing was that as time passed, as quarter ran into halftime and out again, the stands began filling rather than emptying. By the end of the game, when players had moved off to the sidelines, more people were ready for the auction than had come to cheer during the game.

A dozen cars were driven onto the torn and muddied grass, tailgates facing the bleachers. A small wooden stage was erected on the far rim of the cinder track that circled the field itself. A microphone was hooked up. Ms. McCandless climbed onto the stage, dressed in a full-length down coat because Indian summer had disappeared at last. Georgia and a group of her friends hoisted items to be sold up onto the stage's apron so people could get a glimpse of the goods.

After testing the microphone, Ms. McCandless cleared her throat and began. "Ladies and gentlemen, we are here this afternoon to show some friends of ours how we feel about them." She smiled out into the stands and then, after a second, went on. "Many of you have lived in Owanka far longer than I. I hope you won't be offended if I speak for us all now.

"What happened last night was a disgrace. It shamed us all, made us all smaller and less human. We know that we cannot erase the shock and trauma of that, but we want our friends to know that most of us are feeling, sympathetic human beings, honest-to-God caring neighbors in the oldest and truest sense, and that we are not only all lessened by what happened, but also all responsible."

Ms. McCandless was smiling but people in the stands could sense her nervousness. She looked out at them bravely, and seemed for a moment to focus at one section of the crowd. People followed her eyes and found, amid the sea of faces, those of the Brackens: not smiling, standing silently, waiting. Only Charlotte's face had anything resembling an expression, a cross between a rueful grin and a puzzled frown.

"Our auctioneer for this afternoon is Miss Georgia Van Buren, whose hard work and dedication, indeed whose very idea this event is. Georgia?"

Ms. McCandless stepped back and Georgia took her place before the microphone. There was the small sound of gloved hands clapping, and Georgia smiled. Then, typically, without a warm-up of any kind, Georgia lifted a golf bag full of a new set of woods and irons and began to make sounds that resembled an auctioneer's.

Ava and her mother watched from the stands, stamping their feet occasionally to keep warm. They applauded loudly and cheered when, after a few seconds, Georgia had secured a winning bid of one hundred dollars. This was a weak beginning, a bargain, but people needed to be led along, coaxed, urged. They needed to get into the spirit of the moment. The next item, a month's free groceries, went for nearly two hundred dollars to a family large enough to have spent that much weekly. The crowd began to catch on.

Boys on the football team, still in their muddied uniforms, moved among the crowd verifying bids, talking things up, joking and laughing and teasing people into a giving, holiday spirit. Martin took part in this, occasionally glancing at Ava to smile warmly. Louise Nichols took the microphone to give Georgia a rest, accepting each item from Con Arrand or his uncle, who stood nearby. Amos Allen made one of his rare appearances to buy a hand jigsaw for more than he would have paid to buy it at Fred Van Buren's hardware store.

There was an air of determination in all this. People who bid and won items seemed almost to expect congratulations. Many people were genuinely thrilled to have picked up a bargain, or at least to have purchased something at a reasonable price.

But also many were the looks back toward the Bracken family in the stands as the winning bidders climbed down from the bleachers to collect their purchases, looks over a shoulder or a thumbs-up sign that seemed almost pleading—if not for forgiveness, at least for understanding.

Mr. Bracken stood stone-faced throughout the entire auction. His posture was straight, firm, unforgiving. The sun began to sink and he stood yet, a symbol, a totem. He knew this.

His wife sat by his side, nearly invisible, but holding Charlotte's hand. Every so often Charlotte would wave at someone, but that was the extent of her participation.

When the auction was over, a total of fifty-six hundred dollars had been collected. This wasn't enough to buy a new car for the Brackens, but certainly it was an assist.

Mr. Bracken climbed down from the bleachers as people in the stands applauded him. He mounted the small stage to take the microphone. There was an expectant, happy silence that settled over the crowd.

"What's been done here this afternoon," he began in a low, deep, masculine voice, "has made you all feel better, and has reassured my family and me of the good wishes of you all. And we are grateful."

There was a long pause. Then a sort of half smile crossed Mr. Bracken's face and he seemed to catch Charlotte's eye.

"However," he continued, "my family and I would prefer that the money you raised today, instead of being given to us, be donated to the Freedom Is Reading Is Freedom fund."

There was a collective intake of air from the crowd, almost a gasp. Then, after a few more seconds, there was a tiny amount of applause. Without another word from the stage, the stands began to empty and people drifted away from the field toward their homes and cars, walking in little clumps, round-shouldered, some red-faced, others smiling.

The Brackens walked across the grass in the direction of their home, arm in arm, alone, not surrounded any longer by faces or hearts. Mr. Bracken had sliced the single rope that was keeping Owanka at its mooring.

What had been a collective gesture of good will had been turned, again, into politics.

Owanka was adrift.

Chapter 30

"Well, he was obviously upset," said Con Arrand, shrugging off his jacket. He and his uncle had been invited back to the Van Burens' after the auction.

"That's not the point," Georgia said, almost as though she were complaining. "What we did, all of us, people who oppose Mr. Brady and people who support him, was respond as a whole town. It had nothing to do with politics. It was a *human* gesture."

"So, do you feel insulted?" asked Mr. Arrand.

"He was so . . . so stiff-necked!" Georgia said angrily.

"But how can we criticize, Georgia?" said Donald Arrand then. "After all, what he suggested benefits us."

Georgia nodded, brightening. "Well, we can sure use the loot. When I think of Mr. Brady not letting us buy time on his radio station to promote our point of view, I still see red."

"With the money," Con said, "we can print more brochures and flyers and maybe even get an outside speaker for the final rally, and then—"

"Whoa!" said Fred Van Buren, coming into the living-room. "What final rally?"

Mr. Arrand shook his head. "I had hoped that everyone in town knew about that."

"On the night before the election," Georgia explained, "we're going to have a huge torchlight parade and then a rally in the square. Weather permitting, of course."

"What's the point of that?" asked her father. "By then everyone will have made up his mind."

"Not if you read the same paper I do, Fred," said Mr. Arrand. "A lot of people are undecided about the election itself. I suspect on this issue they're also uncertain. A rally will show them that their instincts are right, that they're not alone. It will bolster us at the polls."

"It will?" Georgia's father sounded doubtful.

"Donald?" Mrs. Van Buren came into the room with a tray of cups and coffee, and sandwiches.

"Thank you. We forget every year what the coming of winter feels like."

"You're going to lose," Jonny said then to Mr. Arrand.

"I hope not," replied the older man.

"Look, Jonathan," Georgia said, "everyone has to learn to think for himself. You can't just rely on other people to make decisions."

"What are you talking about?" asked her brother in return.

Georgia blushed but felt committed. "I mean, just because Daddy feels a certain way is no reason you have to automatically agree."

"Now, Georgia," said her mother, "I don't think—"

"Why not?" Jonny demanded. "He's never been wrong before." Then he had another thought. "Besides, Georgia, you've grown up just the way I have. If *you* stopped to think, you'd agree with him, too!"

Having said everything he wanted, Jonny turned quickly to leave the room.

"That seemed unnecessary, Georgia," her mother said quietly.

Mr. Arrand coughed discreetly. "What do you think, Con? Time to head home?"

"Oh, you needn't!" Alva Van Buren said. "Really."

Mr. Arrand smiled and picked up his overcoat. "Thanks so much for the warmth and comfort, Alva. But really, it's time Con and I hit the road." He paused and then grinned. "Besides, we all may have to do battle again tomorrow."

"When will it end?" Ava asked no one in particular. "Even after the election, one side or the other is going to be furious."

"I'm sorry to say I think you're right," Mr. Arrand said, standing near the front door. "Let's just hope it isn't us."

Chapter 31

"Georgia, my love," said her father after the Arrands had left, "if you have a quarrel to pick with me, why not do it directly?"

"Because you don't listen!" Georgia said quickly. "Your mind's made up and that's that. Nothing I or anyone else can say will make a difference!"

"That shouldn't keep you from trying," Fred Van Buren advised.

"Well, it doesn't," Georgia answered. "And you know, Jonny has a point. We've all been taught to believe in the same things. We *should* all see the same threat. Yet there you sit, smug as a bug, determined to vote against me."

Her father smiled. "I'm not voting against you, Georgia. I'm voting against an entire trend in American life of which I do not approve."

"But if I want to read garbage, which I don't know this

book is, who cares? What I read doesn't harm you, does it?"

"The question is, darling, whether it harms you," replied her father. "Look, I'm not saying that later, as you grow, you may not make capable decisions. But now, today, there are children and young people with little experience of the world who can't."

"But, Fred," said Alva Van Buren, "what you're advocating only keeps young people ignorant. It doesn't in the long run make them any more capable of making decisions you approve of."

"How do we learn good from evil?" Ava asked suddenly, having listened patiently with a growing sense of dismay. "If we have no experience of both, how do we recognize them? What kind of parents will Georgia and her friends be if they're not allowed to learn about the world, all of it, the good and the bad?"

"Unfortunately," said her father, standing now and clearly ready to end the discussion, "there is more than enough of both out there, good and bad. And you know what I mean. Exposing people to less of the bad is only a beginning."

"Fred, you can't mean that," said his wife, standing now too. "I mean, that's very close to promoting a benevolent dictatorship."

But Mr. Van Buren had finished arguing. He crossed the room and kissed his wife's cheek. "Come on, sweetheart. Let's take the kids on at Scrabble."

"Scrabble!" Georgia shrieked. "How can you play Scrabble when Rome is in flames?"

Chapter 32

The next morning, Sunday, when Ava came down from her bedroom, her mother had already eaten. For the rest of the family, Mrs. Van Buren had laid out a buffet of scrambled eggs, bacon, muffins, orange juice, slices of melon.

"What's all this?" asked Ava warily.

Her mother smiled. "I don't want to miss a minute of the program," she explained. Then, before she left the room, she caressed Ava's cheek. "It sounded to me, dear, last night, as though you're pretty close to choosing sides, putting your journalistic objectivity aside finally."

Ava shrugged. "Maybe. I'm beginning to realize I do have resources."

"Of course you do," agreed her mother. "That's why Georgia was so clever getting you and that Susan, Susan-what's-her-name, together."

"Susan Woods?" Ava asked, astounded. "You mean Georgia hooked me?"

"Well, I think Georgia knew you were sitting in a pretty powerful spot on *The Hawk*. She didn't think you yourself knew how helpful you could be to the cause."

"It wasn't my cause!"

"Still, Ava," reminded her mother, "this is a good way for you to brighten your chances for college. Ms. Woods understood you had lines into the community she hadn't. Georgia just put it all together."

Ava didn't know what to say.

"It hasn't done you any harm, has it?" asked her mother, standing at the threshold.

Ava sat down at the kitchen table. She had selected no food. "I guess it's been sort of valuable," she allowed. "I mean, I have learned things."

"Well, there you are," decided her mother happily. "You learned more about newspapers and writing. Ms. Woods got an assistant. And Georgia got the issue covered from both angles. I'd say it all worked out for the best."

"Then why don't I feel better about it?"

Her mother smiled nicely. "Maybe because in the middle of this huge crisis, you're having one or two of your own."

"Is that too selfish?"

"No," said her mother firmly. "As a matter of fact, I'd say it's a good sign. It means you're still vulnerable. Stay that way."

Chapter 33

More families than the Van Burens sat before their television sets that Sunday morning watching a newsmaker show on WHO-TV. Later, when Owanka's churches emptied after eleven o'clock services, it was clear from the buzz of parishioners of all persuasions that what they had seen was memorable.

At the Van Burens', the family grouping was varied: Mrs. Van Buren stood, her husband sat in his usual comfortable TV chair, Jonny sat cross-legged at his father's feet. Georgia was as close to the screen as she could be without blocking everyone else's view. Ava sat a little farther back, off to one side, in an easy chair.

Apart from the program's moderator, the cast was made of Joel Claffin, the tenth-grade teacher in whose classes *The Grapes of Wrath* had been tasted; Laura

McCandless, the librarian from Owanka High; Stanley Sopwith; Mrs. George Nichols.

Mr. Claffin, in a gentle, let's-not-give-offense manner, tried to explain how he felt about the battle being waged. "It's so multifaceted," he said. "The freedom to read has become mixed up with God and abortions and foreign policy and farm subsidies. I think people are striking out in frustration. If the times we lived in were better for America, I doubt very much whether we would be facing this choice at all."

"I'd have to argue that," Ms. McCandless disagreed quickly. "There are always people out for power. If you can frighten enough other people, cause them to rely only on your judgments, you can be king of the whole world. What we have in Owanka is a town full of the blind. And a one-eyed man."

"What does that mean?" Jonny asked his father.

Mr. Van Buren smiled crookedly. "'In the city of the blind, the one-eyed man is king.'"

Jonny reflected for a fraction of a second and then laughed. He stood up and left the room to finish dressing for church.

Ms. McCandless sat fidgeting, shaking almost, as she listened to a few seconds of general discussion between the program's moderator and Louise Nichols. Then she burst.

"Mrs. Nichols is being too kind," she said, beginning to let off a full head of steam. "What we're faced with in Owanka is one man's ambition, and the concurrent density of the rest of the population."

She took a big breath. So did the Van Burens.

"This book is not harmful," Ms. McCandless continued swiftly. "It's a classic. But to read it for themselves is too much for our citizens. They'd far rather listen to their friends who—also never having read the thing—believe what they've been told by politicians with axes to grind or, rather, with goals that have little or nothing to do with what most Americans think of as freedom."

"The freedom to protect our children is something we all treasure," Stanley Sopwith broke in.

Ms. McCandless laughed sharply, her image on the state's screens becoming almost angular. "And what about protecting the *rest* of us, *Mr.* Sopwith?" she demanded. "Are *you* getting threatening telephone calls offering to burn down *your* house? Is there hate mail waiting for *you* at the end of *your* hard day's work? Is garbage dumped on *your* lawn while you're sleeping?" She paused to take another big breath. "Was it *your* car that was bombed?"

Mrs. Van Buren and Ava both gasped.

"Are you implying," Stanley Sopwith said, getting even redder than Ms. McCandless, "that Mr. Brady and I are hooligans?"

"Listen, Stanley," Ms. McCandless cut him off. "I can put up with that kind of harassment. I shouldn't have to but I can. And I'm not saying you or Mr. Brady or anyone is directly responsible, just that I thought this sort of election tactic had passed with the Chicago of the thirties."

She leaned forward, closer than before to Stanley. "What I *am* saying is that your side is trying to protect an image of life as you want it to be, not life as it is. Adults get nervous around honesty and guts, and they want their kids equally timid. And if children aren't free to learn about the world in which they're expected to operate as they grow, well, of course, they'll be just as frightened and blinded as their parents."

"Time for church!" Fred Van Buren suddenly announced, standing quickly and turning off the television set with his remote control.

"Daddy!" Georgia wailed. "How can you? That's the most important thing that's ever happened to Owank—"

Her father frowned and cleared his throat. "Not more important, Georgia, than thanking our Creator for His blessings."

Chapter 34

LIBRARIAN DISMISSED

McCandless Forced to Resign

BY SUSAN WOODS

OWANKA, OCT. 27—It was announced last night at the Owanka City Council meeting that the librarian of Owanka High School, Ms. Laura McCandless, an outspoken supporter of FIRIF (Freedom Is Reading Is Freedom) and opponent of the November 6 ballot issue concerning *The Grapes of Wrath,* has resigned her post, effective immediately.

Reached by telephone later, Ms. McCandless viewed her resignation this way.

"I was asked to resign," she told me. "Apparently some remarks made Sunday on WHO-TV were felt offensive by some of the council members. I want people to know that I was firmly supported by Mrs. Louise Nichols, chairperson of the school board committee. And also that I was dismissed not for any dereliction of duty or work deficiency, but purely for personal conviction."

Mr. Fairchild Brady, president of the city council, would make no statement other than to say that a source of "divisiveness within the educational community has been capped."

Chapter 35

Martin Brady and Ava had sat in the jammed Varsity Theater in silence for an hour and a half. While people around them laughed, or wept, at a print of *The Grapes of Wrath* obtained with emergency speed by the enterprising manager of the theater, both Ava and Martin were deep within themselves, weighing and balancing and measuring and regretting or applauding.

The people around them, no matter their sentiments about the upcoming election, found it sad and sobering to see people pushed off their land and forced to flee virtually across the entire continent just on hope, with no money, not enough food, no water to bathe in or to drink, no jobs along the way to help pay for lodging and a little comfort. Henry Fonda was young Tom Joad and Jane Darwell played his mother. Both brought tears to many eyes in the darkened cinema.

When the light came up on the audience, all around them Martin and Ava could see handkerchiefs in people's hands and sense the sadness the story had left them with. The crowd was silent as it filed out of the theater and very few people hung around outside talking afterward. "I don't think this works to your advantage," Martin said as he climbed into his truck.

Ava closed the passenger door. "*My* advantage?"

Martin dodged his implication. "Well, I think it was a good idea to bring in the movie," Martin said, turning his key in the ignition. "But didn't you notice? There were hardly any bad words used. There really wasn't anything that was dirty or perverted or seedy there on the screen."

"But that's good!" Ava objected. "I mean, for all the people who haven't read the book to see there's nothing to be afraid of."

Martin shook his head and smiled rather sadly as they started toward Ava's home. "But, Ava, if millions of dollars were spent bringing the book to the screen, and not one single word or scene was objectionable, that's just more ammunition for my father."

"I don't see that."

"If the story can be told without swear words and dirty things happening, then it could certainly have been told the same way on the printed page," Martin explained. "Dad will just say that if Steinbeck *had* to write this book, this is the way he should have done it." He inhaled. "I think I agree with him."

"What?!" Ava said in an astonished whisper. She turned to stare at Martin. "You agree with your father?"

"Think about it," Martin said. "About what I just said. Doesn't it make sense?"

"It makes sense for a movie but it isn't what the *author* wanted to do."

"That doesn't make any difference," Martin replied.

"Of course it does!" Ava objected heatedly. "You know what movies do to books. I dare you to think of one good movie that was true to what the book's author intended. Hollywood is all happy endings and compromises."

"Not this time."

"Martin, are you telling me you're switching sides?"

Martin shrugged and stayed silent a moment, his eyes deliberately on the road before him.

"Martin?"

"Yes."

Ava sat silently a moment. Then, hoping against hope, she spoke. "'Yes,' as in 'What, Ava?' or 'Yes,' you are changing your mind?"

Martin's hands tightened on his steering wheel. "Yes, my mind is changed."

"Is changed? In cement?"

"In cement."

"After everything you know that's been happening? After people just going about their constitutionally protected activities are bombed and burned? Yes? Yes?!"

"It's a chance you take, being identified with a cause," Martin said a little angrily.

"So, if not the Brackens, then the Van Burens?"

"It could have happened."

"My God, who is this sitting next to me?"

"The same guy who was there a minute ago," Martin answered.

"No, you're not!"

"I am, Ave. I only meant to say that, seeing the movie, well . . . what my dad's saying made sense to me."

Ava was too angry to cry. She felt her mouth dry and her chest grow warm. "Stop this car!" she shouted so suddenly she surprised herself.

Martin did as bid.

Ava pushed open her door and jumped down onto the grass at curbside.

"Hey!" called Martin.

Ava turned. "What?"

"Don't we usually kiss good night?"

"Not anymore! It's too dangerous. You're a carrier of a horrible disease!"

Ava ran into the darkness, steaming. Martin sat a moment in silence, wondering.

Ava rounded a familiar corner and her speed only increased. Her mind was on fire. God, to have found all this out now!

She pulled open her front door. She hurried past her parents, seated watching television, and rushed to her room upstairs. She sat down and took up a yellow pad and pen.

Chapter 36

OWANKA AND THE
EIGHTEENTH CENTURY

Anyone who thinks that the current uproar over *The Grapes of Wrath* is not a matter of personal freedom this week should think again.

Because Ms. Laura McCandless, librarian here at O. High, chose to exercise her constitutional rights of free speech, of viewing life in a different manner, of lobbying for her point of view, she was forced to resign.

Because the family of one of our own students here chose to exercise its right of association and free speech, its car was bombed.

The United States of America was founded by men clear-sighted enough to remember what had brought settlers to these shores originally: dissent, the desire to be free of other people's rules and regulations.

That some of Ms. McCandless's opinions angered certain august citizens of Owanka is clear. What is even clearer is that she is being deprived of her right to earn a living as a free citizen in a democracy because she chose to believe in those rights, for all, including herself.

Because the Brackens embraced the cause of FIRIF, and probably because they are "different," they have been punished anonymously, and in a cowardly way.

The separate ballot measure of November 6 is not simply a matter of protecting Owanka's (ultimately unprotectable) youth from unsuitable literature and language.

It is the first step toward regulating how we all must learn to think and to feel and, finally, to conform to rules of behavior advocated by a small, vocal, and frightened group of people who have forgotten, or are ignoring, the precepts upon which this country was founded.

We sincerely hope that Ms. McCandless will stay in Owanka and continue to fight for what she feels is right.

We hope that Mr. and Mrs. Bracken and their daughter, Charlotte, will be able once again to walk and drive the streets of Owanka with confidence and in a sense of community security.

And anyone who votes on November 6 to curtail their freedoms, or mine, or yours, stands accused herein of betraying our unique and treasured American way of life.

Ava Van Buren

Chapter 37

Oddly, Ms. McCandless's resignation gave people on Georgia Van Buren's team hope.

The unreason of Fairchild Brady, his determination to win at any cost, was exposed. His opponents for city council hammered relentlessly at him for forcing the issue.

Mr. Brady, for his part, sailed on as he had before, calmly, doing his best to disarm his enemies by repeating his argument that taxpayer dollars should not finance corruption and immorality in Owanka's young people.

For many in Owanka, the expectation was that another shoe—perhaps more than one—was yet to drop. Every loud sound, including even a late autumn thunderstorm introduced by sudden peels of distant rumbling, made them tremble, look about, and stop breathing. Some even discussed within their family's havens moving somewhere else. These discussions faded in the knowledge that there really wasn't another town or small city like Owanka that would be free of what Owanka was already experiencing. They would have to stay and do what they could to take their home back to what it had always been considered: green, leafy, friendly, safe.

For all there was relief: the campaign seemed to be winding down. Only two major events were still scheduled for the days before the election: the final rally on its eve, and the decision of churches throughout Owanka to stand publicly on one side or the other.

Since the Reverend Robert Fickett's church had voted to support his letter to *The Owanka Herald* and his public stand—voting against their own fellow parishioner, Fairchild Brady—all denominations decided that they, too, had to step forward to be counted on one side or the other.

There were twelve churches in Owanka to serve a population of slightly more than twelve thousand. Some of these had already announced their feelings about the ballot issue. The Brackens' church, unsurprisingly, supported FIRIF. On the other hand, the Catholics and Mrs. Louise Nichols's own Presbyterians had come down on the opposite side.

At the Van Buren church, during the singing of the opening anthem, "A Mighty Fortress Is Our God," Ava clutched her mother's right hand, and Georgia her left. All three heard the congregation around them singing with resolution and, just below that, a subterranean anger. This was frightening to some, Georgia among them. But in Ava, an exhilaration unknown and unsuspected, reigned.

She realized, even as she wrote her final editorial, that the campaign for FIRIF would keep her from collapsing over the loss of Martin Brady. For the first time since sixth grade, Ava was a free woman, unconnected, alone. She had adored Martin; she had felt confident with him, secure in being part of something others envied.

She imagined that, no doubt on November 7, she would break down and sob.

Yet she felt strangely grateful, relieved in a way to have discovered, even by accident, how fundamentally differently she and Martin saw the world. It was easy for her now to think of him as his father's son, period. She knew this harshness would evaporate with time. She knew she would regret a lot of the things she would lose by being on her own, most importantly Martin's sweetness and strength. But if the latter were founded on a philosophy that seemed, daily, more dangerous and iron-fisted, she would have to tell herself—perhaps many times—that she was better off free.

As the congregation resumed its pews after the hymn, Alva Van Buren sat ramrod straight, looking neither left nor right. Her features were frozen. Ava looked at her and then recalled what she and Georgia had heard from their parents weeks before, as the two of them stood shocked and silently on the porch steps. Mrs. Van Buren was, almost literally, holding her breath.

The pastor threw open the meeting to his parishioners, deferring for once a sermon. Suddenly the vaulted space echoed and rang at such volume it was impossible for all members of the church to hear each speaker. People turned one way and then another, trying to see who was standing, who was speaking, who was waiting to be recognized. But within a short time a free-for-all was in progress.

Man: "What makes you think your kids don't know those words already? Or worse? I mean, who are you protecting?"

Woman: "It's a matter of drawing a line. And as far as I can see, the public purse is as good a place as any to start."

Woman: "This has nothing to do with taxes. It has to do with letting children grow and learn. God knows, we have enough trouble making them study. If they want to read this book, I say let them."

Man: "That's an incredibly stupid attitude."

Woman: "Well, at least it's the way *I* feel, not some bunch of hypocrites a thousand miles away!"

Man: "What's hypocritical about wanting our children to grow into God-fearing, right-thinking citizens?"

Woman: "Besides, it's a chance to stop permissiveness and drugs and . . ."

Man: ". . . bombs?"

Woman: "This is a matter of personal freedom. I wouldn't want my freedom voted on by other people!"

Man: "And are we ready to have the city council come

into our lives to tell us what to do and what not to? I'm certainly not!"

Man: "Yeah, well, it's liberals like you who cry over criminals and then turn around and want the death penalty reinstated."

Woman: "At least I'm not a right-wing bigot who cowers under white sheets!"

Man: "I'd rather have Fairchild Brady running the town than some smart-ass thirteen-year-old!"

"Let us pray!"

It was with nothing but relief that the congregation left the church finally, its secret ballot having been taken. No one cared to stay another second in the angry heat of God's house. They gathered outside to hear the final tally.

Which, when it was announced, caused even more anguish, for the congregants had narrowly voted to support the banning of *The Grapes of Wrath* from the tenth grade.

Arguing began again on the leaf-strewn lawn. The Van Burens did not stay to listen. Following Alva, they turned back toward their home and walked slowly along the roadside.

Suddenly Mrs. Van Buren halted. She stood beneath an emptying cottonwood tree, waiting for the members of her family to surround her. Then she put an arm over Jonny's shoulder and drew him into her body and looked at Georgia and Ava with tear-filled eyes. "I have a confession to make," she said unsteadily.

No one spoke.

"I'm just as bad as Fairchild Brady," Alva Van Buren admitted quietly. "I made your father promise not to speak out at church today. I threatened him. In fact, what I did was censor his right to speak and to be heard. And I am terribly ashamed of myself."

She bent her head and tears appeared on her cheeks.

Fred Van Buren stepped quickly up to embrace his wife. He said nothing, simply holding her, patting her shoulder, kissing her hair.

After a moment more, Alva's sobs softened and finally stopped altogether. She raised her eyes and looked at her husband. He smiled reassuringly, lovingly, and then he turned her around toward home and his family followed silently.

Chapter 38

Suddenly, Owanka seemed to be crawling with even more aliens carrying in what seemed foreshortened arms all kinds of electronic wizardry with which they were able, at a fraction of a second's notice, to record and transmit for posterity the most minute feelings and sensations of the earthlings among whom they walked. Some came harnessed; some wore headdresses that were equipped with their own antennae and lamps, and with all the wires and cables it was clear they were attached, clinging, to some distant Mother Ship to which they could be recalled on the instant.

The Press.

Its attention was not evenly divided between Fairchild Brady's camp and that of Donald Arrand. The real curiosity in the stories these people transmitted was the role of a thirteen-year-old dynamo.

In time, to Ava, it came to seem that as often as Georgia did her single, she and her family minus their father sang backup. Georgia was lit and combed and smiling stage center; behind her, slightly to one side, Ava and her mother swayed with fingers clicking and knees bouncing flexibly, humming doo-wah or oh-yeahs as Georgia sang her verses.

The press was not witness to everything Georgia did or said. For example, there was one grand midnight battle between Georgia and her father over whether she should be allowed some new clothes to match her new persona: Joan of Arc. And there was another set-to between them over whether Fred Van Buren should be allowed to reveal his own sentiments about the election. Wouldn't it, Georgia had demanded, cut the ground out from under her if her own father were seen as opposition? Wouldn't it make her seem less serious and more a child?

Ava thought her father's position a reasonable one. If the story were going to be told, it should *all* be told. Not everyone in town, not everyone in the same family, was obliged to feel identically about *anything*. His point of view was just as valid and just as likely to interest people as Georgia's. After all, he reminded his daughter, without fascists like himself, where would Georgia have found a battle worthy of her?

Ava did not feel the same way about Martin.

Nearly every day the press polled Owanka's citizenry. And the results of these tabulations kept Georgia's spirits high. According to what reporters called their "best information," the populace was almost evenly divided on the book. They noted the way churches had voted, and civic groups. They wondered aloud, on air, about how people would behave once inside voting booths, covered by blue bunting, hidden from the world and alone with their consciences.

In Georgia's mind the certainty grew that in those tiny, enclosed spaces, almost like church confessionals, people would mark their ballots on the side of freedom. There was simply no other choice.

Alva Van Buren gave Georgia a choice: she could have one day off from school. But if she chose Monday, then she had to go back on Tuesday, election day. Which made sense, as far as Georgia could see, for by then, what more could she or anyone else do?

What Georgia accomplished on Monday amazed her family. She was out of the house at dawn, meeting down at the bank with Mr. Arrand and Laura McCandless, planning the route of the parade, which would move from the high school into town. They organized the evening's speakers, arranging who was to follow whom on the podium, worrying over delivery of loudspeaker equipment from Iowa City, working on hand-painted banners and signs for their followers, appointing marshals, filling balloons of red, white, and blue.

At five o'clock, an hour before the march was to begin, Georgia burst back into her house to change into warmer clothes and to collect her speech, on which she had been working off and on for the past week. She bounded down the stairs from her room into the livingroom where her mother had set up a tray-table for her. Mr. Van Buren came back from his store early and was sitting in a wing-backed chair there, drink in hand, as Georgia dove into a plate of spaghetti.

"Is there time for you to give us a preview?" he asked as Georgia began to stuff herself.

Georgia shook her head and swallowed hugely. "You'll just have to come to the rally," she said without a trace of a smile.

"I plan to," said her father.

Georgia nodded curtly, all business.

"Georgia," her father started to say, "I want you to know that no matter what happens, you have my entire admir—"

"I don't want to hear it!" Georgia said angrily, standing up and wiping her mouth with a paper napkin. "I don't want to hear one smarmy word! How my own father can see things this way I'll never know! But I don't want to know now. I give up! If what Ava wrote in *The Hawk* didn't make you change your mind, if Ms. McCandless's being fired didn't do it, if Mr. Bracken's car being blown to bits didn't, then it's clear as can be that nothing can reach you! So just don't try condescending to me now!"

Chapter 39

Georgia grabbed her coat, which was festooned with buttons and campaign badges, and ran from the room without looking back. The door behind her slammed.

And she crashed right into Con Arrand.

"Hey! Take it easy," Con said, his arms around Georgia to keep her from falling.

When she looked into his eyes, hers were tear-filled.

"What's the matter?" Con asked sympathetically, lowering his arms after another second.

"I don't want to talk about it!"

Con smiled. "Come on, Georgia."

Georgia tried to push past him. But Con grabbed at one of her hands and forced her to walk down the steps carefully, and to begin to walk toward the headquarters for the march slowly.

"What is it?" he asked again.

Georgia just shook her head.

"Well, then," Con decided, "I'll talk for a while. O.K.?"

Georgia nodded, hardly looking at her friend.

"I heard from my father today," Con said.

"And?"

Con laughed. "Boy, when you're not interested in something, you really aren't!"

"I'm interested," Georgia admitted, plowing straight ahead. "What did he say? When do you leave?"

"I don't have to."

Georgia stopped dead. "What?"

Con grinned. "I don't have to leave, Georgia."

"But I thought—?"

Con nodded. "That's what we've done before, always. When he and Mom get settled, I get a tutor or they find me a good school, and I join them."

"But now?"

"Now, my dad's decided it makes more sense for me to stay with Uncle Don."

Georgia couldn't help herself. She was beginning to feel better. She was beginning to smile, just barely.

"You see, Dad's a sort of trouble-shooter. He gets assigned places to go, usually about every two years. He goes off, talks to people, tries to settle them down, tries to get them to see what America has in mind. How it can benefit them.

"But this time, looking ahead, Dad thought I might want to stay here and finish high school. After all, I'm an American. I should have some American friends, shouldn't I?"

"I think so," Georgia said slyly.

Con laughed softly. "So do I."

The two began again to walk hand in hand toward Georgia's destination.

"So," Georgia said after a moment, "what are you going to do?"

"Stay. I can visit Mom and Dad on vacations. Uncle Don has agreed to keep me as long as I want to stay."

Georgia nodded, smiling to herself, still striding determinedly forward.

"Georgia?"

But Georgia didn't answer. She knew if she did, if she stopped for even a second, she might be rewarded with the first real serious kiss of her life. And she wanted that, desperately.

Instead, she clasped Con's hand more tightly and pulled him along. After all, she had a job to do. The kiss would be her reward.

She stopped. If she'd been thinking in words, she would have asked herself, Why wait?

She turned to Con quickly and raised her face.

Chapter 40

The Van Buren house was halfway between down-town Owanka and its high school. No one had far to walk, or to return if he tired and wanted to, an option that appealed to Ava because the weather had grown cold and windy and snow flurries were forecast for the area. Jonny had chosen to stay at home. "I'll probably see you on TV later, anyway. Why freeze?"

As the three remaining Van Burens neared the athletic field behind Owanka High, they could hear the murmur of the crowd, a steady growing hum that rose and fell and rose again. But how big the crowd was none had antici-pated.

As they rounded a corner of the school and looked at the field past the bleachers, there were a thousand people. Old people, middle-aged, schoolchildren, par-ents, gaggles of teens. Mr. Arrand and Georgia and Ms.

McCandless and Mrs. Nichols milled among the throng, distributing buttons and streamers and balloons and banners, encouraging their troops, smiling and laughing and giving thumbs-up signs in the gathering darkness. Suddenly a whistle was blown and people obediently quieted and maneuvered into position.

The march began, flashlights and burning torches held in the air, banners blowing in the breeze, campaign badges and buttons reflecting the firelight. There was an atmosphere of expectation, the thrill of being surrounded by so many people who believed and cared about the same thing. Whenever a television cameraman's lights played over the marchers, shouts rose and arms waved in the air and people chanted "Freedom Is Reading Is Freedom, Freedom Is Reading Is Freedom!"

The three Van Burens walked arm in arm amid the mob, located about a third of the way back in the train. Her mother was chanting along with the rest of Georgia's followers, her voice reaching an easy sing-along. She looked very beautiful to Ava: her face flushed, her eyes bright. Ava saw in her what her father must have twenty years earlier.

The crowd of marchers was perhaps half a mile from the town square when it saw the opposition, much of it silent, lining the roadway. Many of these nodded silently at friends or family members who passed, but there was no other greeting before they too turned to follow the march. Ava was at first fearful this was done to intimidate. She saw placards about abortion and Right to Life movements and immigrants and taxes.

The marchers rounded a corner and found themselves in the center of the square, being drawn magnetically to the steps of city hall, its white columns lit by floodlights as well as by the smaller, more precise lights of television cameramen. A stage had been erected there on the steps and it was lined with red, white, and blue bunting and balloons. Microphones stood ready and switched on and when Donald Arrand mounted the few steps to stand before the crowd and raise his hands over his head, the roar that erupted from his cohorts rang out to be amplified by them and then to ring back in their ears from the loudspeakers strategically placed around the approach to city hall.

The chanting of "Freedom Is Reading Is Freedom" continued for a minute or slightly more. The marchers were encircled by hundreds of other people clearly not in sympathy with their cause.

After a few words of welcome, to *all,* Mr. Arrand began to warm up his supporters. "Now I know that people have tried to confuse the issue here. Have tried to make those of us who favor the freedom of children to read into godless, pro-abortion wastrels of the public purse. Have tried to intimidate us by violence. But we stand here tonight simply to show them, and anyone else who may be watching, what freedom really means. It includes the right of assembly!" A solid wall of applause rose. "It includes the right of choice, whether that choice be religious or political or personal!" More applause greeted his words. "It affirms the professionalism of our teachers and leaders of our young who want only to be allowed to do the best possible job under what are frequently the least advantageous of circumstances." Still more applause rang.

Fred Van Buren applauded politely, clapping his gloved hands a few times and nodding as though he had been in agreement all along. Ava looked at him quickly and punched his elbow. Her father leaned toward her. "He's right, after all. Freedom does include those things."

Georgia assumed Mr. Arrand's place at the microphone. She stood modestly waiting for the crowd to quiet. She did nothing but stand absolutely still, a smile on her face, waiting. When finally all was silent, she took one more step toward the microphone. With her arms still at her sides, and without gestures, she spoke into the bulb of the microphone clearly. Her voice sounded very, very young, but also idealistic, determined, jubilant.

"If you would," she began, "you're invited to repeat after me a sort of pledge I believe all members of FIRIF can support." She paused. "I am an American," she announced proudly. "An American is free to choose . . ." She waited. After a hesitant start the crowd collectively agreed to follow her direction.

". . . where he lives," Georgia said strongly. The crowd echoed her.

". . . with whom he lives."

"With whom he lives."

". . . at what he works and where."

"At what he works and where."

". . . to worship in his own church."

"To worship in his own church."

". . . his own friends and neighbors."

"His own friends and neighbors."

". . . to speak the ideas of his mind, and the longings of his heart."

"To speak the ideas of his mind, and the longings of his heart."

". . . to profit by the lessons of others."

"To profit by the lessons of others."

". . . and to learn to live, to love, to be an American from any source he can."

"And to learn to live, to love, to be an American from any source he can."

"Thank you very much," said Georgia then, backing away from the microphone and sitting down.

There was a second's silence and then a thunderous cry of support erupted. People cheered and clapped and stamped until Louise Nichols stood to take the microphone in *her* hand.

"I won't take much of your time," she began. "It's too chilly."

"Right on!" someone shouted from below her.

"Before we introduce the candidates for city council we support, and who support FIRIF, I want to tell you that this country got where it is by keeping its eye on the ball. And that's what we're doing here tonight. We don't want to argue with our friends about economics or national prestige. All we want is the right of our children to learn about the world."

Mrs. Nichols smiled at the nods and applause from the crowd. "What we want is clean, moral, and honest. It's called freedom!"

A burst of voices cheering broke over the square. Ava felt exhausted.

When Mrs. Nichols had introduced the eight candidates for the council that FIRIF supported, Laura McCandless stepped to the microphone. There was a rush of whispering and then applause which started slowly and built. Had people been seated they would have risen to their feet. She waited patiently, smiling, competent and cool. After a moment she raised her hands just a little to ask that the applause stop. It did.

"My name," she said clearly, "is Laura McCandless. I was librarian at Owanka High."

The applause began to rise again. But Ms. McCandless cut it short. "I am not a martyr. None of us here is. All I am is a citizen of this country who expects that the guarantees in our Constitution reach out to include herself. As they do you . . . and your children."

Before renewed support could escalate, she continued quickly. "We at Owanka High take, or took, our responsibilities seriously. We examined and read every book we recommended or approved or bought. We brought the best and clearest sets of standards we could to these decisions, teachers and librarians alike. As professionals, we want to do our job well, we want to help

initiate children into a meaningful and worthwhile adult-
hood."

She smiled then. Ava felt relieved. Suddenly the event
had become almost too heavy to bear.

"The freedom to read is a precious one," Ms. McCandless said after a moment. Her voice began to quaver.
"Don't let angry, ambitious, ignorant people take it away
from you or your children!"

Half a dozen people started to clap but Ms. McCandless was not finished. She was shaking now, and tears
were beginning to fall from her eyes.

"No matter how hard we try," she said, almost shouting now, "in the face of prejudice and racism and intol-
erance, we cannot fight alone!"

Her shoulders were heaving. Ava and her mother,
along with hundreds of others, held their breath.

"Don't let this country down! Don't give in to hate-
mongers! Don't give in to ambitious, unprincipled dem-
agogues who try to make you afraid and ashamed to
exercise your rights as Americans!"

There was total silence as Ms. McCandless then
slumped back into the shadows and stood before her
chair, sobbing uncontrollably.

*No wonder she's a wreck . . . she's lost her job, been threatened
and bullied . . . stood up to it all . . . she had to crack some time . . .
there is a difference between the abstract and the personal . . . she's
been mutilated by all this . . . here is Owanka's first walking-
wounded . . . the poor woman.* Ava tore off her gloves and
started to clap. Her mother did the same, both of them

hoping to send Ms. McCandless a message that some people in the crowd understood her pain and were sympathetic.

Within a few seconds, others in the crowd also sent the same message. There were no cheers, no shouts. This reaction was more dignified, more aware, more purposeful. The ovation continued.

Mr. Arrand stepped toward the microphone and then abruptly turned back away from it again, motioning for Ms. McCandless to come forward.

She did, but reluctantly, standing at Mr. Arrand's side, unable to look out at the crowd. Tears still streamed down her cheeks.

The crowd's hands would not be stopped. Finally, though, Ms. McCandless was allowed to disappear once more into the shadows at the back of the stage. Then Georgia and Mrs. Nichols joined Mr. Arrand at the microphone. They seemed to be speaking in unison, and at first the crowd could not hear their words: "My country, 'tis of thee, Sweet land of liberty . . ."

By the time the trio had reached "Of thee I sing," the crowd was with them. The anthem rose through the night air and seemed weighted with what perhaps was the crowd's first realization that it was, indeed, in a battle for part of its freedom.

The singing was solemn, not elated, and when, at the end of the song, Mr. Arrand stepped forward and leaned down into the microphone to say, "Thank you all for coming," they knew how horrible war could be.

Chapter 41

"I'm going into the kitchen," Fred Van Buren announced, "and make as much popcorn as the biggest pan will hold. I am going to melt a pound of real butter—cholesterol be damned!—and then I'm going to come back here to offer it to you. You had better be smiling."

"Fat chance," said his wife under her breath. Then she smiled. "I'll do it, Fred. You stay and watch the returns." She stood up.

"Ohhh, Alva," said her husband.

"Don't you 'ohhh, Alva' me," Mrs. Van Buren replied quickly. She and her husband exchanged looks and then both laughed.

Ava sat with her father, switching between a fairly local station (there wasn't one that belonged to Owanka alone) and the networks for state and city returns. Neither Ava nor her father made comment when a checkmark was placed beside a name or a proposition that had been chosen by voters.

It seemed that all of Owanka had voted early, and already on the radio there were projections of winners and losers. While the issue of *The Grapes of Wrath* was still in doubt, the races for the city council seemed to have been decided quickly and decisively. Martin's father was out.

"Can I come down?" Jonny yelled from the upstairs hallway.

"No," called his father. "Tomorrow's a school day and you already know who's going to be president."

"I can smell popcorn!" Jonny shouted.

"It's bad for your digestion!" his father yelled in return. Then he gave in, as Jonny must have known he would. "Go back to bed. I'll bring some up when it's ready."

On the screen before them, Ava and her father watched as another moderate senator failed to be re-elected. From the kitchen they could hear, "Damn!"

"I can still smell it!" Jonny shouted from his bedroom.

"I'm coming, I'm coming!" his father called back. "Keep your shirt on!" He stood and went toward the kitchen quickly, returning with a cereal bowl full of popcorn, which he carried upstairs to his son.

"You know," said Ava's mother, standing and leaning against the doorway to the kitchen, "I can understand returning Irene Clarke. And I'm pleased Louise Nichols scraped by. And even Stanley Sopwith, bless his soul." She laughed. "And I *mean* that, Ava. The poor man, taken over by the rabid right. He won't be able to move without finding a sword in his ribs."

"It's not as though he wouldn't deserve it," Ava said as her mother came farther into the livingroom and sat on a couch. "You know, there *isn't* any sex between animals and human beings in that book."

"I know that."

"I wonder why no one ever called him on it."

"How many people would go to the trouble of reading the book?" her mother asked in return.

"Any sympathy for Mr. Brady?" Ava ventured.

"Not one whit! Fairchild doesn't need to be on the council anyway. He's got more than enough influence in this town."

"Still, I wonder why he lost."

"The same reason, partly, that Amos Allen lost. People like change," Alva replied. "Also, in Fairchild's case, the way he treated Ms. McCandless. Not to mention that I think he made a mistake trying to stay above the battle. I mean, after all, he started it. You can't do something like that and then pretend that to be involved is somehow beneath you."

Mr. Van Buren reappeared and sat beside his wife as the returns flashed before them all. They watched without comment as reporters spoke about the early presidential decision, about various governors' races, about state and local issues. Then suddenly, on the screen, on national television, came the Owanka vote projection for *The Grapes of Wrath* proposition.

The network must have had a direct line into Owanka's city hall because as each ballot was tallied, it appeared in the count.

"Oh no," whispered Ava.

The count had just become 1649 for the proposition to ban the book, 1618 against.

It was less the numbers that appeared on the screen that all three Van Burens worried over. It was what they would mean, and do, to Georgia.

Time passed, and the huge container of popcorn emptied. Then, without warning, the front door slammed, startling everyone.

Georgia appeared on the threshold, her face tear-streaked and pale, her mouth trembling.

"Darling!" her mother said, standing up quickly to embrace her.

But Georgia ducked and took a step away, shrugging off her parka at the same time. She took a few steps into the livingroom and stared at her father. "Well," she shouted, "are you happy?"

"Not to see you this way, sweetheart."

"Well, you made me this way!" Georgia cried out.

Her father started to stand and go to Georgia but she motioned she didn't need that. He stopped and after a silent moment he resumed his place on the sofa. "I certainly had a hand in making you," he said after another pause. "But at a certain point, one should be old enough to accept responsibility for what one becomes."

"Oh, smooth!" Georgia declared. "That's the whole trouble, you know. All the way through this thing, you've been so laid back, so cool. You're exactly like the others."

Her father smiled. "No better, no worse," he admitted. "But you're not losing by a landslide, darling. It's still very close. You did a spectacular job."

"But don't you realize what you've done?" Georgia demanded. "You voted against democracy!"

Mr. Van Buren scavenged in the popcorn bowl. "Listen to yourself, please. I voted—*in* a democracy, Georgia. Pure and simple. I did my civic duty, gladly, proudly. Other people voted as I did, and some differently. What you're so steamed up about is that democracy has just shown you it can contain ideas *you* don't approve of."

"Georgia," said her mother gently, "stop a minute and think what you've done. Think what you were able to accomplish. There ought to be some pleasure in that."

Georgia spun. "Well, there isn't!"

Alva Van Buren shook her head. "I'm sorry about that, sweetheart. Really. You have won the respect of *so* many people."

"I can't live in a house where people don't believe in freedom!"

"Mother voted for your side," Ava inserted.

"Of course she did! She at least has brains and a sense of history!"

"And I don't," her father asked without adding a question mark.

"Well, how can you? Anyone could see that what was

at stake here was continuing what America is based on. I mean, you're so all-fired hot to return to the good old days, you forgot what the good old days were."

"I'm not sure that's true," answered her father. "But I do know I don't like the tone of voice you're using."

Georgia lowered her voice, a little. "Well, just how, and why, do you think the Van Burens ever came over here anyway?"

Fred Van Buren shrugged. "I imagine some of their friends talked them into it."

"Well, I certainly hope not!" Georgia snorted. "I hope at least someone in this family understood what was going on."

"A lot of people agreed with you, remember," Ava suggested.

"I can't play a numbers game!" Georgia declared.

"It's very difficult discussing this, then, dear," said Georgia's mother, "when no matter what we say, or how much sense it makes, you always have an answer."

"What did you expect?" Georgia demanded. "I've just spent almost three months of my life, my whole *youth,* fighting for what I believe in."

"It was a good fight," her father soothed. "You've nothing to be ashamed of. You nearly won."

"I am *not* ashamed!" Georgia announced. "Far from it. I'm going to fight for the rest of my life."

"For what?" Ava asked.

"For people against a wall, being mistreated, being bullied by power and influence and money."

"You don't have to do that alone," her father said.

"I know that!" Georgia snapped. "If nothing else, all this has shown me I'm *not* alone, even though my very own family wouldn't support me."

"Mother's right," Ava said then. "This is a no-win argument."

Georgia inhaled hugely and stood straight. "You may as well know right now that this battle isn't over! Mr. Arrand says we can take this to court, we can appeal, find it unconstitutional. And that's exactly what we're going to do! Other people, other towns have. So," Georgia said, scooping up her parka and getting ready to leave the room, turning to make her curtain speech, "from now on I'm on my own! You can advise and talk and worry, but I'm no longer a child! And you'd better realize that!"

Alva Van Buren looked at her husband as Georgia ran up to her room. "Has there been much doubt of that lately?" she asked.

Fred Van Buren smiled in return. "Of course, dear, *our* side has not yet begun to fight."

"God, Fred, if you tell Georgia that, she'll murder you in your sleep."

Her husband laughed. "It wouldn't be nearly as much fun for Georgia if she didn't have opposition."

"Oh Lord!" Alva sighed. "I thought I knew my family!"

"I'm teasing, honey," Fred said.

"Thank God for that!" his wife said happily, but with a tiny trace of worry still in her voice.

"Well," Ava announced, standing up, "she's all yours. I think I'll go out into the world to see what *other* battles are being fought."

Her mother smiled. "Well, dear, if I know Georgia— and I admit I may not, after all this—if ever you run into another war, don't be too surprised to find her in the front lines."

Ava nodded and grinned. "Probably somewhere behind me."